Reeds in the Wind

Reeds in the Wind

Grazia Deledda

Translated by Martha King

Introduction by Dolores Turchi

ITALICA PRESS
NEW YORK
1999

Italian Original
Canne al vento

ITALICA PRESS, INC.
595 Main Street
New York, New York 10044

Library of Congress Cataloging-in-Publication Data
Deledda, Grazia, 1871-1936.
[Canne al vento. English]
Reeds in the wind / Grazia Deledda ; translated by Martha King ; introduction by Dolores Turchi.
p. cm.
ISBN 0-934977-63-1 (alk. paper)
I. King, Martha, 1928- . II. Title.
PQ4811.E6C213 1998
853'.8--dc21 97-32515

Printed in the United States of America
5 4 3 2

Editorial/Production Assistant: Elizabeth McKeegan.
Cover Illustration: Italica Press Archives.

Introduction

The themes that appear in *Reeds in the Wind* are not exclusive to life in Sardinia, the island of Grazia Deledda's birth. They are eternal themes: the cycles of guilt, expiation, forgiveness that occur in every life, everywhere. Perhaps for this reason it is one of her most popular novels and the one the writer loved best.

Grazia Deledda wrote *Reeds in the Wind* after she had lived in Rome for many years. Therefore, the places and the characters from her earlier days became memories veiled by nostalgia for a land far away, in spite of the fact that its inhabitants were always severe in their judgments of her. When barely launched on her writing career the harsh criticism of relatives and townspeople of Nuoro had blocked her literary vocation for some time. Good girls did not write stories and novels to be published for all the world to read, whose characters could be cause for ridicule. Neither were they impressed that her ambitions for herself were combined with a desire to help her island so neglected by the rest of Italy. In spite of it all, Deledda never forgot the great silences and beautiful, wild landscapes of her land, the character and primitive beliefs of the inhabitants, and she continued to draw from that fund of memories.

Reeds in the Wind is set in Galtellì (Galte in the novel), a small town in the region of Baronia, a short distance from the eastern coast of the island, and not far from larger Nuoro. There the Pintor women live, whose family was once great landowners, but who are now reduced to a decaying house and small farm. They remain rooted in the old snobberies that make them different from the poor inhabitants of the community and therefore unable to adapt to a changing society. These sisters, Noemi, Ruth, and Ester (Lia escaped long ago) prefer to isolate themselves in a scornful reserve, cultivating the values and memories of another time. Efix, their farm tenant, has remained with them as a way to expiate a sin he had committed many years before.

Efix is representative of Deledda's protagonists who are reminiscent of the old patriarchs, repositories of an ancient wisdom that goes back to Biblical times and the sayings of Solomon. Words put into the mouths of these wise, natural men, such as Efix, reflect the beliefs of her native region, Barbagia – a belief system that evoked the Old Testament God, a God more just than loving.

To Efix's strength and spirit of resignation is contrasted the weakness of the Pintor women's nephew, Giacinto, who continually oscillates between duty and pleasure. His arrival in Galte revives old guilts and new temptations and sets the fatal drama into motion.

Galte, in the early twentieth century, is cursed with the evils that had plagued Sardinia for ages: the nightmare of malaria; the extreme poverty of the villages of Baronia, subjected to nature's atmospheric whims; and the continual struggle to defend the cultivated land from the frequent floods that often destroyed everything in their path, leaving behind desolation and death.

Such grim descriptions alternate with depictions of a landscape that Deledda draws from her vivid memory, creating stupendous scenes that are illuminated by bright sun or moonlight almost as in a fable. Also like fairy tales seem the beliefs of popular imagination, the dark beings who populate the Sardinian nights, the tiny fairies who live in caves and rocks, the sprites with seven red caps who bother sleep.

With the colors of nostalgia Deledda paints that fantastic atmosphere in which her characters move, especially in descriptions of country festas that became a parenthesis of joy and happiness, a yearly pause in the fatigue of the daily grind. These religious feasts were not only a time for devotion, but were also a time for enjoyment and social interaction, animated by dancing, music, singing and the bright colors of the local costumes.

In such festas Noemi, the younger of the Pintor sisters, does not participate in her later years. She lives within the walls of her house as in a kind of prison where few are allowed to enter, so that they will not see how far the Pintor family has fallen. A voluntary prison that separates her from the flow of life, sacrificing her on the altar of a nobility that has no reason for existing.

Reeds in the Wind is a novel where tragic events are consumed in silence: desperate secrets torment the characters until death. Scrabbling for the merest existence never ends, pride does not yield even in the face of necessity, guilt is silently expiated and can be forgiven only by voluntary submission and harsh mortification to the Divine Judge, the only one Sardinians truly accept and respect.

The art of Grazia Deledda developed out of an authentic writing vocation that inspired her to see the events of life as tragic destinies so often weighing people down. More often than not the individual is helpless to resist providence.

The human frailties and fatalism typical of Deledda's characters are well summarized in the phrase the writer puts in the mouth of the principal protagonist, Efix: "We are like reeds in the wind. We are the reeds and fate is the wind."

Reeds in the Wind is pervaded by an instinctive lyricism that merges with strong passions, transforming them into song, or as Deledda herself wrote, into "a motif that springs spontaneously from the lips of a primitive poet."

— Dolores Turchi

I

Efix, the Pintor sisters' servant, had worked all day to shore up the primitive river embankment that he had slowly and laboriously built over the years. At nightfall he was contemplating his work from where he was sitting in front of his hut halfway up white Doves' Hill. A blue-green fringe of reeds rustled behind him.

Silently stretching out before him down to the river sparkling in the twilight was the little farm that Efix considers more his than the owners': thirty years of possession and work had certainly made it his, and the two hedgerows of prickly pear that enclose it like two gray walls meandering from terrace to terrace, from the hill to the river, are like the boundaries of the world to him.

In his survey the servant ignored the land on either side of the farm because it had once been Pintor property. Why dredge up the past? Useless regret. Better to think about the future and hope in God's help.

And God promised a good year, or at least He had covered all the almond and peach trees in the valley with blossoms; and this valley, between two rows of white hills covered with spring vegetation, water, scrub, flowers, together with the distant blue mountains to the west and the blue sea to the east, gave the impression of a cradle billowing with green veils and blue ribbons, with the river murmuring monotonously like a sleepy child.

But the days were already too hot and Efix was also thinking about the torrential rains that swell the bankless river and make it leap like an all-destroying monster. One could hope, but had to be watchful, like the reeds along the riverbank beating their leaves together with every breath of wind as though warning of danger.

That was why he had worked all day and now, waiting for night, he wove a reed mat so as not to waste time and prayed that God make his work worthwhile. What good is a little embankment if God's will doesn't make it as formidable as a mountain?

Seven reeds across a willow twig, and seven prayers to the Lord and to Our Lady of Rimedio, bless her. In the intense twilight blue her little church and the quiet circle of cabins around it down below lay like a centuries-old abandoned prehistoric village. At this hour, as the moon bloomed like a big rose in the bushes on the hill and euphorbia spread its perfume along the river, Efix's mistresses were also praying. Donna Ester, the oldest, bless her, was certainly remembering him, the sinner. This was enough to make him feel happy, compensated for his efforts.

Footsteps in the distance made him look up. They sounded familiar. It was the light, swift stride of a boy, the stride of an angel hurrying with some happy or sad announcement. God's will be done. It's He who sends good and bad news; but Efix' heart began to pound, and his black cracked fingers trembled on the silvery reeds shining in the moonlight like threads of water.

The footsteps were no longer heard. Nevertheless, Efix remained motionless, waiting.

The moon rose before him, and evening voices told him the day had ended: a cuckoo's rhythmical cry, the early crickets' chirping, a bird calling; the reeds sighing and the ever more distinct voice of the river; but most of all a breathing, a mysterious panting that seemed to come from the earth itself. Yes, man's working day was done, but the fantastic life of elves, fairies, wandering spirits was beginning. Ghosts of the ancient Barons came down from the Castle ruins above Galte on Efix's left and ran along the river hunting wild boar and fox. Their guns gleamed in the short alder trees along the riverbed, and the faint sound of barking dogs in the distance was a sign of their passing.

Efix could hear the sound that the *panas* – women who died in childbirth – made while washing their clothes down by the river, beating them with a dead man's shin bone, and he believed he saw the *ammattadore* (the elf with seven caps where he hid his treasure) jumping about under the almond woods, followed by vampires with steel tails.

It was the elf that caused the branches and rocks to glitter under the moon. And along with the evil spirits were spirits of unbaptized babies – white spirits that flew through the air changing themselves into little silvery clouds behind the moon. And dwarfs and *janas* – the little fairies who stay in their small rock houses during the day weaving gold cloth on their golden looms – were dancing in the large phillyrea bushes, while giants looked out from the rocks on the moon-struck mountains, holding the bridles of enormous horses that only they can mount, squinting to see if down there within the expanse of evil euphorbia a dragon was lurking. Or if the legendary *cananèa*, living from the time of Christ, was slithering around on the sandy marshland.

During moonlit nights especially this entire mysterious population animates the hills and valleys. Man has no right to disturb it with his presence, just as the spirits have respected him during the sun's course; therefore it's time to retire and close one's eyes under the protection of guardian angels.

Efix made the sign of the cross and stood up, but he was still waiting for someone. Nevertheless he shoved the plank that served as a door across the entry way and leaned a big reed cross against it to keep spirits and temptation from entering his hut.

Through the cracks the moonlight illuminated the corners of the low, narrow room – but a room large enough for someone like him who was as small and scrawny as a young boy. From the conical cane and reed roof over the dry stone walls, with a hole in the middle for the smoke to escape, hung bunches of onions and dry herbs, palm crosses and blessed olive branches, a painted candle, a scythe for keeping vampires away, and a little sack of barley for protection against the *panas*. With every breath of air everything quivered and spider webs shone in the moonlight. On the floor a two-handled pitcher lay on its side, and a pan rested upside down next to it.

Efix unrolled his mat but didn't lie down. He thought he kept hearing the sound of a boy's footsteps. Someone was certainly coming, and in fact dogs on nearby farms suddenly began to bark, and the whole countryside, which a few moments earlier seemed to sleep amid prayers murmured by nocturnal voices, was full of echoes and rustling almost as though it had suddenly jerked awake.

Efix pushed the plank aside. A black figure was coming over the rise where the low bean plants grew silvery under the moonlight, and he, to whom even human shapes seemed mysterious at night, made the sign of the cross again. But a voice he recognized called out to him. It was the clear but slightly breathless voice of the boy who lived next door to the Pintor sisters.

"Zio Efisè, Zio Efisè!"

"What's happened, Zuannantò? Are the women all right?"

"They seem all right to me. They sent me to tell you to go to town early tomorrow, because they need to talk to you. Maybe it's because of the yellow letter I saw in Donna Noemi's hand."

"A letter? Do you know who it's from?"

"I don't know. I don't know how to read. But grandmother says maybe it's from their nephew, Giacinto."

Yes, Efix felt it had to be. Nevertheless, head down, he thoughtfully rubbed his cheek, and hoped and feared he was wrong.

The tired boy sat down on a rock in front of the hut and unlaced his boots, asking if there was something to eat.

"I ran like a deer. I was afraid of the spirits...."

Efix raised his olive-colored face, hard as a bronze mask, and gazed at the boy with his little bluish eyes, deep set and surrounded by wrinkles. Those lively, shining eyes were full of childish anxiety.

"They said for me to go to town tomorrow or tonight?"

"Tomorrow, I told you! I'll stay here to guard the farm while you're in town."

The servant was accustomed to obeying the women without asking questions. He pulled an onion from the bunch, a piece of bread from his bag, and while the boy ate, laughing and crying from the sharp onion, they began to talk. The town's most important people entered their conversation. First came the Rector, then the Rector's sister, then Milese who had married a daughter of the Rector and had gone from hawking oranges and amphoras to being the richest merchant in the village. The mayor, Don Predu, came next, the Pintor sisters' cousin. Don Predu was also rich, but not like Milese. Then came Kallina the usurer, she also rich, but in a mysterious way.

"Thieves tried to break down her wall. Impossible. It's bewitched. And she was laughing this morning in her courtyard, saying: even if they get in they'll only find ashes and nails, poor as Christ. But my grandmother says that Zia Kallina has a little sack of gold hidden in the wall."

These stories were really of little interest to Efix. Lying on his mat, with one hand tucked under his arm and the other on his cheek, he felt his heart beating, and the reeds rustling on the riverbank sounded like an evil spirit sighing.

A yellow letter! An ugly color, yellow. Who knows what had happened to those women. For twenty years whenever some event broke the monotonous life at the Pintor house it was inevitably a disaster.

The boy also lay down, but he didn't feel like sleeping.

"Zio Efix, just today my grandmother said that the Pintors were once as rich as Don Predu. Is that true?"

"It's true," the servant said with a sigh. "But now's not the time to be thinking about these things. Go to sleep."

The boy yawned. "But my grandmother said that after saintly old Donna Maria Cristina died she walked around her house like an excommunicated soul. Is that true or not?"

"Go to sleep, I say. Now's not the time...."

"Let me talk! Why did Donna Lia run away? My grandmother says you knew about it and you helped her, you went to the bridge with Donna Lia where she hid until a cart came by that would take her to the sea to get on a boat. And that her father Don Zame looked for her till he died. He died there, by the bridge. Who killed him? My grandmother says you know...."

"Your grandmother is a witch! She and you, both of you, should leave the dead in peace!" shouted Efix; but his voice was hoarse and the boy laughed insolently.

"Don't get mad 'cause it's not good for you, Zio Efix! My grandmother says a goblin killed Don Zame. It that true or not?"

Efix didn't answer. He closed his eyes and put his hand over his ear, but the boy's voice buzzed in the dark and it sounded to him the voice of spirits from the past.

Little by little they all gathered around him, entering through the cracks like moonbeams: Donna Maria Cristina, beautiful and calm as a saint; Don Zame, red and violent as the devil; their four daughters whose pale faces have the serenity of their mother and their father's flame in the depths of their eyes; maidservants and menservants, relatives, friends – everyone who invades the rich house of the Barons' descendants. But once the wind of misfortune blows, people disperse like little clouds around the moon when the wind blows off the mountains.

Donna Cristina dies; her daughters' pale faces lose some of their serenity, and the deep flame in their eyes grows. It grows to such a degree that after his wife's death, Don Zame becomes as domineering as his Baron ancestors, and like them keeps his four daughters shut up in the house like slaves while they wait for husbands worthy of them. And like slaves they had to work, make bread, weave, sew, cook, know how to take care of their things. But above all they couldn't raise their eyes to men, or even allow themselves to think about anyone not destined to become a husband. But the years went by and the husbands didn't come along. And the older his daughters became the more Don Zame expected them to adhere to a strict manner of comportment. If he saw them at the windows overlooking the lane behind the house or if they went out without his permission, he would slap them and shout insults, while threatening death to the young men who passed by on the lane more than twice in succession.

Don Zame spent his days roaming around town or sitting on the stone bench in front of the shop belonging to the Rector's sister. When people saw him they would slink away, afraid as they were of his tongue. He quarreled with everyone, and was so envious of others that when he passed by a nice farm he would say, "may lawsuits devour you." But lawsuits ended up devouring his land, and an unspeakable catastrophe struck him suddenly like punishment from God for his pride and his prejudices. His third daughter, Donna Lia, disappeared one night from the paternal house and nothing more was known about her for a long time. A deathly shadow fell over the house. Never had the town known such a scandal; never had such a noble and well-brought up young woman like Lia run away like that. Don Zame seemed to go mad; he ran around here and there searching for Lia all over the Baronia district and along the Coast; but no one could give him any information. At last she wrote her sisters saying she was safe and happy to have broken her chains. However, her sisters didn't forgive her or answer her. Don Zame became even more tyrannical. He sold what was left of his inheritance, mistreated the servant, annoyed half the world with lawsuits, kept traveling in the hopes of tracking down his daughter and bringing her back home. The shadow of dishonor over him and his entire family because of Lia's flight weighed on him like a cloak of the damned. One morning they found him dead on the bridge outside town. A stroke must have killed him, because there was not a sign of violence – only a small green mark on the back of his neck.

People said that maybe Don Zame had quarreled with someone who had struck him with a walking stick. But in time this rumor faded and the certainty prevailed that he had died of a broken heart over his daughter's leaving.

While her sisters, dishonored by her escape, were unable to find husbands, Lia wrote announcing her marriage. Her husband was a cattle dealer that she had met by chance. They lived at Civitavecchia, were comfortably well off, and would soon have a child.

Her sisters did not forgive her this new wrong: marriage with a common man met in such a sorry manner. They did not reply.

Some time later Lia wrote announcing Giacinto's birth. They sent a present to their little nephew, but didn't write his mother.

The years went by. Giacinto grew up, and every year he wrote his aunts at Easter time and Christmas, and his aunts sent him a present. Once he wrote that he was studying, another time that he wanted to join the navy, and still another time that he had found a job; then he wrote about his father's death, then his mother's, and finally he expressed the desire to visit them and settle down if he could find work in town. He didn't like his job with the Customs Office: it was menial and tiresome, a waste of his youth. Of course he loved to work, but out in the open. Everyone advised him to go to his mother's island and try his luck with an honest job.

His aunts began to talk it over, and the more they talked the less they agreed.

"Work?" said Ruth, the calmest sister. "If the little town can't provide work even for those who were born here?"

Ester, on the other hand, was sympathetic with their nephew's plans; while the youngest, Noemi, smiled coldly and scornfully.

"Perhaps he thinks to come here to play the gentleman. Come right ahead! He can go fishing in the river...."

"He says he wants to work, Noemi! Then he'll work: he might be a trader like his father."

"He needs experience first. Our family has never dealt with cattle."

"In the past, dear Noemi! Nowadays gentlemen are merchants. See Milese? He says he's the Baron of Galte now."

Noemi laughed with an evil look deep in her eyes, and her laugh was more discouraging to Ester than all her other sister's arguments.

Everyday it was the same story: Giacinto's name resounded throughout the house, and even when the three sisters were silent he was in their midst, as he had always been anyway from the day he was born, his unknown shape filling the decaying house with life.

Efix didn't remember ever taking part directly in their discussions. He didn't dare. First of all because they didn't consult him, and then not to have qualms of conscience. But he wanted the boy to come.

He loved him. He had always loved him like a member of the family.

After Don Zame's death, Efix had remained with the three women to help them settle their tangled affairs. Their relatives didn't care about them, they even held them in contempt and spurned them. The sisters were only capable of domestic tasks and knew nothing about the little farm, their last remaining inheritance.

"I'll stay another year in their service," Efix had said, moved to pity by their helplessness. And he had stayed twenty years.

The three women lived on the income from the farm he cultivated. In lean years, Donna Ester would say to Efix when the moment came to pay him (thirty scudi a year and a pair of boots): "Be patient, for the love of God. You'll get what's coming to you."

He was patient, and their debt to him grew year after year, so much that Donna Ester, half joking, half serious, promised to leave him the farm and house, although he was older than they. Old now, and weak, but he was still a man, and his shadow was still enough to protect the three women.

Now it was he who dreamed about good fortune for them. At least that Noemi might find a husband! What if the yellow letter brought good news, after all? What if it was about an inheritance? What if it was a marriage request for Noemi? The Pintor sisters still had rich relatives living in Sassari and Nuoro. Why couldn't one of them marry Noemi? Don Predu himself could have written the yellow letter....

And there in the servant's tired imagination things have suddenly changed as from night to day; everything is light, sweetness. His noble mistresses have become young again, they rise on wings like eagles taking flight; their house rises up from ruin and all around everything blooms again like the valley in spring.

And for him, the poor servant, there's nothing left to do but retire to the little farm for the remainder of his life, to spread out his mat and rest with God, while in the silence of the night the reeds whisper the prayer of the sleeping earth.

II

Efix left at daybreak, leaving the boy to guard the farm.

The road went uphill all the way to town, and he walked slowly because the year before he had had an attack of malaria and his legs were still weak. Every once in a while Efix stopped and turned to look back at the farm all green between the cactus walls. And the hut, black among the blue-green reeds and the white rock, seemed like a nest to him, a real nest. Every time he left it he looked back at it like that, tender and sad, just like a migrating bird. He felt like he was leaving the best part of himself there, the strength that gave him the solitude, the detachment from the world. And going along the road up through the scrub land, he felt like a pilgrim with the woolen *bisaccia* – the woven length of material with pockets that served as a saddle bag or knapsack – over his shoulders and an alder stick in his hand, headed toward a place of punishment: the world.

But may God's will be done and let's keep on going. Suddenly the valley lies before him, and at the crest of the hill (the hill itself like an enormous heap of ruins) appears the Castle ruins. An empty blue window like the eye of the past looks out upon the melancholy panorama reddened by the rising sun: the undulating plain with sandy gray scrub, yellowish rushes, the greenish vein of the river, the little white villages with a bell tower rising out of the center like the pistil of a flower, the mountains above the villages, and in the background a mauve and gold-colored cloud over the Nuorese mountains.

Efix keeps walking, small and dark amid the luminous grandeur. Oblique sun rays make the whole plain sparkle. Every rush has a thread of silver, from every euforbia bush rises a bird cry. And over there the sun-striped, shadow-plowed green and white cone of Mount Galte; ahead the town like ruins of an ancient Roman city: deteriorating low stone walls, roofless stone houses, remnants of courtyards and stone barricades. Inhabited hovels, even more melancholy than the ruins, flank the sloping roads that are paved with massive sandstone in the center. Volcanic rocks lying about give the impression that a cataclysm had destroyed the old town and scattered its inhabitants. A few new houses surrounded by pomegranate and carob trees rise shyly out of such desolation. Groups of prickly pear and palm trees add a poetic note to the dreary scene.

But the further Efix goes up the incline the more dismal it becomes, and crowning it all are the remains of an ancient cemetery and a Pisan-style basilica in ruins, in the shadow of the mountain, among blackberry bushes and euforbia. The roads were deserted and boulders on the peak of Monte now looked like marble towers.

Efix stopped in front of a large door adjacent to that of the ancient cemetery. The two doors were nearly alike, each preceded by three broken, grass-invaded steps. But while the door of the ancient cemetery was a dilapidated, weathered plank, the door belonging to the three women had a masonry arch and in the architrave were remains of a coat of arms: a helmeted warrior's head and an arm with sword. The motto read: *Quis resistit hujas?*

Efix crossed the wide square courtyard paved with flat sandstone like the roads, grooved for draining rainwater. He took his *bisaccia* from his shoulders, looking around to see if one of his mistresses were there. The two story house faced the courtyard, right in front of Monte that seemed to hang over it like an enormous green and white hood.

Three small doors were below a wooden balcony that wrapped around the upper story, reached by an outer staircase in poor repair. A blackened rope, knotted and held by pegs substituted for the missing railing. The doors, supports, and banisters of the balcony were in finely sculptured wood; everything, however, was in such poor condition that the rotted, blackened wood looked like it might crumble into powder at the slightest provocation, as though attacked by an invisible auger.

However, here and there on the balcony banisters, in addition to the slender, still intact columns, were the remains of cornices with a decoration of leaves, flowers and fruit in relief. Efix remembered that balcony awakening a religious respect from the time he was a boy, like the pulpit and balustrade around the Basilica's altar.

A short, heavy woman, dressed in black with a white kerchief around her dark, hard face, appeared on the balcony. When she glanced down and saw the servant her dark, almond-shaped eyes sparkled with joy.

"Donna Ruth, *padrona mia, buon giorno!*"

Ruth hurried down, unmindful that her thick legs covered with dark blue stockings might be seen. She smiled at him, revealing strong teeth under a dark, downy upper lip.

"And Donna Ester? Donna Noemi?"

"Ester has gone to mass. Noemi just got up. A nice day, Efix! How's the farm doing?"

"Fine, fine, thanks be to God. Everything's fine."

The kitchen was also medieval: large, low, beamed ceiling blackened by smoke; a carved wooden chair against the wall, a large fireplace; through the barred window the green background of the mountain. On the bare, reddish walls were the signs of missing copper pots; and the smooth, shiny pegs which once held saddles, *bisacce*, weapons, seemed to have been left there in their memory.

"Well, then, Donna Ruth?...." Efix asked, while the woman put the little copper coffee pot on the stove. She turned her large dark face, framed in white, toward him and motioned for him to be patient.

"Go get some water while we wait for Noemi to come down...."

Efix took the bucket and started out, but turned shyly at the door, looking down at the dangling bucket.

"Is the letter from Don Giacintino?"

"Letter? It's a telegram...."

"*Gesù grande*! Nothing bad has happened to him?"

"Nothing, nothing! Don't worry."

It was useless to keep asking before Noemi came down. Although Ruth was the eldest of the three sisters and kept the keys to the house (there was nothing else to be in charge of), she never took any initiative or responsibility on her own.

He went over to the well that looked like a *nuraghe* in the corner of the courtyard, protected by a rock wall on which yellow gillyflowers and jasmine grew in old broken pitchers. One of the jasmine bushes had climbed up the wall and looked out at the world to see what was there.

This corner of the courtyard, gloomy with moss and happy with the polished gold of gillyflowers and tender green jasmine, stirred so many memories in the servant's heart!

He still seemed to see Donna Lia on the balcony, pale and thin as a reed, her eyes fixed on the distance, she too wanting to see what was going on in the world. The day of her escape he had seen her like that, standing immobile up there like a ship's captain who explores the mysteries of the sea with a glance.

How heavy these memories were! Heavy like the bucket full of water tugging down, down in the well.

However, raising his eyes, Efix saw that the tall woman on the balcony hooking the sleeves of her long black jacket wasn't Lia.

"Good morning, Donna Noemi! Aren't you coming down?"

She bowed slightly, her thick dark hair shining around her pale face like two strips of satin; she returned his greeting with eyes also dark and shining under long lashes, but she didn't speak and she didn't come down.

She opened the doors and windows wide – anyway there was no danger of a breeze slamming them and breaking the glass (missing for so many years!) – and brought out a yellow blanket to hang in the sun.

"You're not coming down, Donna Noemi?" Efix repeated, looking up from under the balcony.

"Now I am."

But she continued to carefully spread out the blanket and seemed to be contemplating the melancholy beauty of the panorama left and right: the sandy plain divided by the river and rows of poplar trees, low alders, rows of reeds and euforbia; the Basilica overgrown with black brambles, the ancient cemetery where white bones lay like margaritas on the green weeds. And in the background the hill with the Castle ruins.

Golden clouds crowned the hill and ruins, and the morning sweetness and silence lent a sepulchral serenity to the whole landscape. The past still ruled; the bones of the dead seemed its flowers, the clouds its diadem.

Noemi was not disturbed by this. As a child she had grown accustomed to seeing the bones that seemed to be warming in the sun in the winter and that glistened with dew in the springtime. No one ever thought about removing them. Why should she? Ester, however, coming slowly and calmly up the road from the new village church (when she was in the house she was always rushing about, but outside she did things calmly because a noble woman must be calm and tranquil), made the sign of the cross and prayed for the souls of the dead when she reached the ancient cemetery.

Ester never forgets anything and nothing ever escapes her observation: so, as soon as she reaches the courtyard, she notices that someone has drawn water from the well and put the bucket back in its place. She removes a stone from a vase of gillyflowers and goes into the kitchen. Greeting Efix, she asks him if they have given him coffee.

"I've already had it, Donna Ester, *padrona mia*."

In the meantime Noemi had come down with the telegram in hand, but had not yet made up her mind to read it, almost as though she took pleasure in exasperating the servant's anxious curiosity.

"Ester," Noemi said, sitting on the bench next to the fireplace, "why don't you take off your shawl?"

"They're saying mass in the Basilica this morning. I'm going out again. Read it."

Ester sat down on the bench and Ruth did the same. Seated thus the three sisters resembled one another in an extraordinary way, except that they represented three different ages: Noemi still young, Ester middle aged, and Ruth already old, but a strong, noble, serene old age. Ester's eyes, a little lighter than her sisters', of a golden nut color, had a childlike and mischievous glint.

The servant stood in front of them, waiting. But after unfolding the yellow paper Noemi looked at it almost as though she couldn't decipher the words, and finally shook it crossly.

"Anyway, it says he'll be here in a few days."

She raised her eyes and blushed as she stared at Efix. The other two were looking at him also.

"Do you understand? Just like that. Nothing more, almost as though he were coming home!"

"What do you say about it?" asked Ester, hooking a finger in her crossed shawl.

Efix looked happy. The thick wrinkles around his bright eyes looked like rays and he didn't try to hide his joy.

"I'm just a poor servant, but I say providence knows what it's doing!"

"Thank the Lord! There's at least one person who understands the reason," Ester said.

Noemi turned pale. Words of protest rose to her lips, and even though she managed, as always, to control herself in front of the servant whom she seemed to give little importance, she couldn't keep from replying: "Providence has nothing to do with it. That's not what this is about. It's a matter.... " After a moment's hesitation, she continued, "It's a matter of telling him right out that we have no room for him in our home!"

Then Efix opened his hands and bent his head slightly, as if to say: then why ask me? But Ester began to laugh and stood up, impatiently pulling the two black wings of her shawl together.

"And where do you want him to go, then? To the Rector's house like strangers who can't find a room?"

"I wouldn't even answer him," suggested Ruth, taking from Noemi's hand the telegram that she kept nervously folding and refolding. "If he comes, welcome. He should be received just like a stranger. Welcome, guest!" she added, as though greeting someone who had come in the door. "All right. And if he doesn't behave himself there is always time for him to leave."

But Ester was smiling, looking at the most timid and irresolute of the three sisters. She bent over and slapped Ruth on the knee: "Time to chase him off, you mean? What a fine scandal that would cause, dear sister. And would you have the courage to do it?"

Efix was thinking. Suddenly he raised his head and rested a hand on his chest.

"You can leave that to me!" he promised heartily.

Then his eyes met Noemi's, and he who had always been afraid of those cold, limpid eyes like deep water, understood that the young employer had taken his promise seriously.

But he wasn't sorry about making that promise. He'd taken on some awesome responsibilities in his lifetime.

Efix stayed in town all day. He was worried about the farm – even if by that time there was little to steal – but he felt that a hidden disagreement was troubling his mistresses, and he didn't want to leave before seeing their differences settled.

Ester, after straightening up some things, went out again to attend mass at the Basilica. Efix promised to join her, but when Noemi went upstairs, he went into the kitchen and in a low voice begged Ruth, who was kneeling on the floor kneading dough on a low table, to give him the telegram. She looked up, and with her hand white with flour, pulled it from her kerchief.

"Did you hear her?" she said quietly, nodding in the direction of Noemi. "It's always her! She's ruled by pride."

"You're right!" agreed Efix thoughtfully. "A noble is always noble, Donna Ruth. Did you ever find a buried coin? It looks like iron because it's black, but if you polish it you see it's gold.... Gold is always gold...."

Ruth realized it wasn't necessary to excuse Noemi's exaggerated pride with Efix, and always ready to go along with the opinions of others, she cheered up.

"Do you remember how proud my father was?" she said, picking up the white dough in her red, blue-veined hands. "He used to talk that way, too. He wouldn't have let Giacintino get off the boat. What do you think, Efix?"

"Me? I'm just a poor servant, but I'd say Don Giacintino would get off just the same."

"His mother's son, you mean?" sighed Ruth, and the servant sighed, too. The shadow of the past was always there, surrounding them.

But the man made a gesture as though to chase away this shadow, and his calm returned as he watched her red hands pulling, folding, beating the white dough,

"The boy's clever, and providence will help him. But be careful he doesn't get the fever. And, of course, you'll have to buy him a horse, because they're not used to walking on the mainland. I'll take care of it. The important thing is for you women to get along."

But she said immediately, proudly: "Don't we get along? Have you ever heard us argue? Aren't you going to mass, Efix?"

He understood that she was dismissing him and went into the courtyard, but he looked around to see if he could also speak to Noemi. There she was now, taking the blanket off the balcony. No use asking her to come down, he'd have to go up to her.

"Donna Noemi, may I ask a question? Are you happy?"

Noemi looked at him in surprise, the blanket in her arms. "What about?"

"Don Giacintino coming. You'll see, he's a good boy."

"And when did you meet him?"

"I can tell by the way he writes. He'll be able to do a lot. You'll have to buy him a horse, though...."

"Oh, yes, and spurs, too!"

"...Everything depends on you women getting along. That's the main thing."

She picked a thread off the blanket and tossed it into the courtyard, a sullen look on her face.

"When haven't we gotten along? Always, up to now."

"Yes...but...it seems like you aren't happy about Don Giacinto coming."

"Do I have to sing? He's not the Messiah!" she said, passing sideways through the little door through which could be seen a white room with an antique bed, an antique chest, a small paneless window showing green Monte in the background.

Efix went down the stairs, picked a little pink gillyflower, and holding it in his fingers laced behind his back, set off for the Basilica.

The silence and coolness coming off Monte was everywhere. Only a titmouse warbling in the brambles broke the silence, accompanied by the monotonous prayer the women intoned in the church. Efix entered on tip toe, the flower in his fingers, and knelt behind a pulpit column.

The Basilica had deteriorated; everything was gray, damp, and dusty. From holes in the wooden roof rained oblique rays of silvery powder that fell on the kneeling women. And the yellowish figures that leaped from the black, cracked backgrounds of paintings still decorating the walls resembled these women dressed in black and violet, each pale as ivory, even the most beautiful, the most refined, with thin chests and stomachs swollen by malarial fevers. The women's prayer had a slow and monotonous resonance like a distant vibration beyond time. The mass was for the dead, and a gold-fringed black cloth covered the altar balustrade. The priest in black and white turned slowly with his hands raised, two rays of light dancing around him as though emanating from the head of a prophet. If the little sacristan hadn't rung the bell that seemed to drive spirits away, Efix could have believed he was attending a mass for ghosts in spite of the light and the birds singing. They were all there: Don Zame kneeling at the family pew, and behind him Donna Lia, pale in her black shawl like the figure in the ancient picture that the women look at now and then and that seems to be looking out from a black, crumbling balcony. It is the figure of the Magdalene painted, they say, from life: love, sadness, remorse and hope laugh and cry in her deep eyes and bitter mouth....

Efix looks at her and, as always when facing this figure looking out from the dimness of an infinite past, feels his head spinning as though he is suspended in a black, mysterious void.... He can almost remember an earlier, very remote life. It seems that everything around him is alive, but with the fantastic life of legend. The dead are revived, Christ behind the yellow altar curtain (on display only twice a year), comes down from His hiding place and walks. He, too, thin, pale, silent. He walks and the people follow him, and in the middle of everyone is he, Efix, who walks endlessly, the flower in his hand, his heart agitated by a rush of tenderness.... The women sing, the birds sing. Donna Ester walks next to the servant with her fingers clasping her crossed shawl. The procession goes outside town, and the town is all in flower with pomegranates and buttercups. The houses are new, the Pintor family's shining walnut front door is new, the balcony is intact.... Everything is new, everything beautiful. Donna Maria Cristina is alive and watches from the balcony where silk blankets are hanging. Donna Noemi is very young, engaged to Don Predu, and Don Zame, also following the procession, pretends to be worried as always, but is very happy....

The women stopped singing and got up to leave. Efix, who had been resting his head against the column of the pulpit, shook himself out of his dream and followed Donna Ester home.

The high sun now beat down on the little town, more than ever desolate in the blinding light of the already hot morning. The women leaving church dispersed, silent as ghosts, and everything was once again solitude and silence around the Pintor sisters' house. Donna Ester went to the well to cover a little carnation plant, and then went quickly up the steps to close the windows and doors. The banisters creaked at her steps and a powder like gray ash rained down from the wall and rotted wood.

Efix waited for her to come back down. Sitting on the steps in the sun, with the peak of his cap folded forward to shade his face, with his jack knife he sharpened a peg that Donna Ruth wanted in the portico; but the flash of the blade in the sun hurt his eyes and the little wilted flower trembled on his knees. He felt confused and remembered the fever that had plagued him last year.

"That devil coming back?"

Donna Ester came down, with a little cork vase in her hand. He moved aside to let her pass and raised his face shaded by the cap.

"You're not going out again?"

"Where do you think I'd be going at this hour? No one has invited me to dinner."

"I'd like to ask you something. Are you happy?"

"What about, my friend?"

She treated him maternally, without familiarity, however; she had always considered him a simple man.

"That...that you're all in agreement about Don Giacintino coming?"

"Yes, I'm happy. That's the way it has to be.

"He's a good boy. He'll do well. He'll have to have a horse. But...."

"But?"

"He can't have too much freedom in the beginning. Boys will be boys.... I remember when I was a boy, if someone let me squeeze his little finger I would twist his whole hand. And then, the Pintor men, you know...Donna Ester...are proud...."

"If my nephew comes, Efix, I'll talk to him like a guest: sit down, make yourself at home. But he'll understand he's a guest here...."

Efix stood up, brushing wood shavings from his arm. Everything was going well, and yet he felt uneasy. He had something else he wanted to say, but didn't dare.

He followed the woman, taking off his cap to give him more strength to drive the peg in, patiently waiting until Donna Ester filled the bucket with water.

"Give it to me!" he said, taking the bucket from her, and as he pulled up the water he looked into the well to avoid looking her in the face, since he was ashamed to ask for the money she owed him.

"Donna Ester, I don't see the bundles of reeds any more. Does that mean you sold them?"

"Yes, I sold some of them to a Nuorese, and had some put on the roof, so I also had to pay the mason. You know that the wind blew tiles off on the last day of Lent."

He let it go, then. There are many ways to set things right without humiliating the people you love! So he went to Kallina the usurer, stopping first to speak to the grandmother of the boy staying at the farm. Tall, thin, with her Egyptian face framed by a black kerchief, the angles folded back over her head, the old woman sat spinning on the steps of her dark stone hovel. A string of coral hung on her long, yellow, wrinkled neck; two gold pendants at her ears trembled like luminous drops that couldn't decide to fall. It was as though she had forgotten to take off these jewels of her youth as she grew old.

"Ave Maria, Zia Pottoi. How's it going? The boy stayed up there, but he'll be back this evening."

She looked at him with vitreous eyes.

"Oh, is that you Efix? God help you. Well, who's the letter from? From Don Giacintino? If he comes treat him right. After all, he's coming home. It's Don Zame's soul, because the souls of the old live again in the young. Look at my granddaughter Grixenda! She was born sixteen years ago, on the feast of Christ, while her mother was dying. Well, look at her. Isn't she her mother all over again? Here she is...."

Here, in fact, was Grixenda coming back from the river with a basket of clothes on her head. Tall, with her skirts raised above her shining, straight deer-like legs. And resembling a deer's were her wide, humid eyes in her pale face like an ancient medallion. A red ribbon criss-crossed her open bodice, supporting her young breasts.

"Zio Efix!" she shouted, roughly and affectionately, putting the basket on his head while she rummaged in his pockets. "My good soul! I'm always thinking of you, and you have nothing for me.... Not even an almond!"

Efix let her go on, cheered by her gracefulness. But the old woman, with her immobile face and glassy eyes, said sweetly:

"Don Zame is coming back."

Then Grixenda stiffened, and her pretty face and eyes vaguely resembled her grandmother's. "Coming back?"

"Stop that kind of talk!" Efix said, putting the basket down at the girl's feet, but she was listening as though enchanted by her grandmother's words.

Even as he went on down the street he thought he saw the past at every corner. Over there, sitting on the stone bench against Milese's gray house, was a large man dressed in velvet, the brown hue emphasizing his red face and black beard.

Wasn't it Don Zame? He stuck his chest out the same, his thumbs in his vest pockets, his red fingers laced with his gold watch chain. He stays there all day watching the passersby and making fun of them. Many go down another street for fear of him, and Efix does the same to reach the usurer's house unseen.

A hedge of prickly pears surrounded Zia Kallina's courtyard like a thick wall. She was also spinning. Tiny, with embroidered shoes, stockingless, with her little white face and gilded eyes like a bird of prey glittering in the shadow cast by her kerchief.

"Efix, dear brother! How are you? And your little women? What brings you here? Sit down, sit down, rest awhile."

Sleepy chickens pecking under their wings, happy kittens running beside rosy piglets, white and bluish doves, a donkey tied to a post, and swooping swallows gave the courtyard the appearance of Noah's ark. Her little house stood in the shadow of the old Milese house – a tall house with a new roof, but with the plaster peeling away as though defaced by a wrathful time jealous of those who try to protect its prey.

"The farm?" Efix said, leaning against the wall next to the woman. "It's fine. This year we'll have more almonds than leaves. I'll be able to pay you everything, Kallì! Don't worry."

She wrinkled her bare brow, her eyes following the thread of her spindle.

"Wouldn't think of it! Look, I wish everyone were like you, and the seven scudi you owed me were a hundred!"

"You witch!" thought Efix. "You gave me four scudi at Christmas time and now it's already seven!"

"Well, then, Kallì," he said in a low voice, bowing his head as though he were talking to the piglets busily sniffing at his feet. "Kallì, give me another scudo! Then that makes eight, and in July, sure as the sun, I'll give it back to the last centesimo."

The usurer didn't answer, but looked him over from head to foot and then stretched out her fist in an obscene gesture.

Efix was startled and grabbed her wrist, while the piglets ran away followed by the kittens, and the hens squawked at such confusion.

"Kallì, damn it, if it weren't for men like me, you'd be fishing for leeches instead of practicing usury."

"Better to fish for leeches than let men like you suck my blood! Yes, fool, I'll give you the scudo; I'll give you a hundred and ten, if you want them, like I give to others more respectable than you, to your mistresses, to the nobles, and to the Barons' relatives, but I'll give you the finger as long as you're stupid, that is until the day you die.... I'll give them to you...."

And she went to get five silver liras.

Efix went away with the money in his fist, followed by the woman's ironical salutations.

"Tell your mistresses to take good care of them."

But he had decided to put up with anything in order to make a good impression for Don Giacintino's arrival. He wanted to buy a new cap to welcome him, and so he went to Milese's shop, even resigned to greeting the man on the bench. It was Don Predu, the Pintor sisters' rich relative.

Don Predu replied with a haughty lift of his head, but he wasn't too proud to overhear what the servant wanted to buy.

"Give me a cap, Antoni Franzì, a long one and without moth holes."

"I didn't get it from the Pintor house," answered Milese, who had a biting tongue. From outside Don Predu cleared his throat as a sign of approval, while the shopkeeper climbed up a step ladder.

"Everything grows old and everything is renewed, like the year," replied Efix, his eyes following Milese's thin figure still dressed in the long fur overcoat of his home town.

It was a small shop, but crammed tight. The shelves were red with scarlet piece goods and next to that the glittering green of bottles of mint. Sacks of flour pushed their white paunches up against the black humps of the herring barrels, and in the little window naked women on illustrated postcards smiled at vases of stale almond-covered candies and rolls of faded ribbon.

While Milese dragged long black caps from a box and Efix measured the circumference with his open hand, someone opened the little door leading to the courtyard, and in the vine-wreathed background appeared an imposing woman on a long bench spinning calmly as an ancient queen.

"That's my mother-in-law. Ask her if these caps didn't cost me nine *pezzas*," Milese said, while Efix tried on one of them, pulling it down on his forehead and folding the tip back over his head. "You've chosen the best one. You aren't as simple as they say! Don't you see it's a wedding cap?"

"It's tight."

"Because it's new, God bless you. Take it. Nine *pezzas*: that's like throwing it in the street.

Efix took it off and stroked it thoughtfully. Finally he put the usurer's money on the counter.

Don Predu stuck his head in the door, and the fact that Efix was buying such a luxurious cap had also attracted the attention of Milese's mother-in-law. She called the servant with a motion of her head and solemnly asked him how the Pintor women were. After all they were noble women and merited the respect of decent people. Only successful merchants like her son-in-law Milese could be disrespectful.

"Give them my greetings and tell Donna Ruth I'll come visit them soon. Donna Ruth and I have always been good friends, even if I'm not of nobility."

"You have a nobility of soul," Efix replied gallantly, but she gave the spindle a light spin as though to say, "that's enough of that!"

"Even my brother the Rector thinks highly of your mistresses. He always asks me: "When are we going to the feast of Our Lady of the Rimedio with the Pintor sisters again?....

"Yes," she went on in a nostalgic tone, "we all used to go to the feast together when we were young. It didn't take much to entertain us. At that time people seemed ashamed to laugh."

Efix carefully folded his cap. "God willing, this year my mistresses will go...to pray and not to enjoy themselves."

"That will be nice. Tell me something, if you can. Is it true that Lia's son is coming? They were talking about it in the shop this morning."

Because Milese had come closer to the door and was laughing at something Don Predu said under his breath, Efix exclaimed with dignity: "It's true! I'm in town just because I have to buy a horse for him."

"A stick horse?" Don Predu asked, laughing uproariously. "Oh, that's why I saw you leaving Kallina's den."

"What's she got to do with it? We've never asked her for anything!"

"Of course, fool! You'd never get anything from me! Except a piece of good advice! Leave that boy where he is!"

But Efix walked out of the shop with his head high, his cap under his arm, and he went away without a reply.

III

However, the next few days, and for entire weeks, the Pintor sisters waited in vain for their nephew.

Ester made bread just for the occasion, white and thin as a holy wafer, the kind usually made only for festivities. She also secretly bought a basket of cookies. After all, a guest was coming and hospitality is sacred. Every night Ruth dreamed about their nephew's arrival, and every day around three, the hour the coach came, she would spy from the doorway. But the hour went by and everything was quiet.

Early in May Noemi was alone in the house because her sisters had gone to the feast of Our Lady of Rimedio, as they did every year from time immemorial – for penitence, they said, but also a little for diversion.

Noemi didn't care for either, and yet, while she sat in the hot shade of the house on that long luminous afternoon, she nostalgically followed her sisters' trip in her mind. She could see the little church, gray and round like a big upside-down nest in the middle of the wide, grassy courtyard, the ring of stone cabins inside of which were squeezed people as many-colored and picturesque as a tribe of gypsies; the primitive, colonnaded belvedere above the priest's cabin, the blue background, the whispering trees, and the sea sparkling down below amid silvery dunes. Thinking about these sweet things made Noemi feel like crying, but she bit her lip, ashamed of her weakness.

Every year spring gave her this restless feeling: life's dreams blossomed in her again, like roses among the tombstones of the ancient cemetery. But she knew it was only a short-lived weakness destined to end with the first warmth of summer, and she let her fantasy roam, incited by the same calm drowsiness that languished around her, in the courtyard red with poppies, on Monte shaded by passing clouds, over the entire village, half of whose inhabitants were at the feast.

In her thoughts she was down there, too.

She seems to be a girl again, on the priest's belvedere on a May evening. A great copper moon rises from the sea and the whole world seems made of gold and pearl. An accordion fills the air with plaintive cries. The courtyard is illuminated by a fire's rosy gleam that makes the slender figure of the dark musician and the purplish faces of the women and children dancing the *ballo sardo* stand out against the gray wall. Their shadows move like phantoms on the trampled grass and along the church walls; gold buttons, silvery braids of costumes, accordion keys flash and gleam. Everything else is lost in the pearly shadows of moonlight. Noemi remembered never taking part directly in the feast, while her older sisters laughed and enjoyed themselves, and Lia crouched like a hare in a grassy corner of the courtyard, perhaps thinking of escape even then.

The feast lasted nine days, the last three becoming a continuous circle dance accompanied by songs and music. Noemi always stayed on the belvedere among the banquet remains. Around her sparkled empty bottles, broken plates, some apples of an icy green color, a platter and a forgotten little spoon. Even the stars moved over the courtyard as though struck by the rhythm of the dance. No, she didn't dance, she didn't laugh, but it was enough for her to see people enjoying themselves, because she too hoped to take part in the festival of life.

But the years passed and the festival of life took place far from the little town, and in order to be a part of it her sister Lia ran away from home....

She, Noemi, remained on the crumbling balcony of the old house just as she had once stood on the priest's belvedere.

Toward sundown someone knocked at the front door she always kept locked.

It was the old Pottoi woman, come to ask if she needed her services. Without waiting for an invitation from Noemi she sat on the ground with her back to the wall, and loosening the kerchief from her bejeweled neck, she began to talk longingly about the religious festival.

"Everyone is down there. Even my grandchildren, may Our Lady help them. Oh, everyone is down there and keeping cool, because it's by the sea."

"Why didn't you go, too?"

"And the house, Donna Noemi? No matter how poor you are, you can't leave a house completely alone. Otherwise a sprite might set himself up in it. The old stay home, the young go out!"

She sighed, looking down at herself to rearrange the corals on her breast, and told about when she, too, went to the feast with her husband, her daughter, her good neighbors. Then she raised her eyes and looked toward the ancient cemetery.

"I seem to see all the dead from those days. They all went down there to enjoy themselves. I can still see your mother, Donna Maria Cristina, sitting on the bench in the corner of the big courtyard. She was like a queen with her yellow skirt and black embroidered shawl. And the women from so many villages and towns sat around her like servants.... She said to me: 'Pottoi, come here, have some coffee. What do you think – is it good?' Yes, that's how humble she was. Oh, that's why I don't want to go back there. I feel like I've left something there I'll never find again."

Noemi nodded vigorously, her head bent over her work. The old woman's voice was like the echo of her past.

"And Don Zame, Donna Noemi? He was the soul of the feast. He often ranted and raved like a tornado but after all he was really good. There's always a rainbow after a storm. Oh, yes, even now when I'm down there spinning, I seem to hear a horse pass by.... It's him, going to the festival on his black horse, with his *bisacce* stuffed full.... He greets me as he goes by: 'Pottoi, want to get on the rump? Climb up, old girl!'"

She imitated the voice of the dead man. Then, suddenly, following her thoughts, she asked: "Isn't Don Giacintino still coming?"

Noemi stiffened because she couldn't allow anyone to mix in her family affairs.

"If he comes he'll be welcome," she answered coldly; but as the old woman went away Noemi again took up the thread of her thoughts. She lived so much in the past that the present hardly interested her any more.

The more the hot shade from the house extended over the courtyard and the odor of euphorbia came from the plain, the more intensely she remembered Lia's flight. It's a sunset like this one. White and green Monte looms over the house, the sky is golden. Lia paces silently back and forth in her room. She comes to the balcony, pale, dressed in black, her dark hair catching the gilded blue of the sky. She looks down there toward the Castle, then suddenly lifts her heavy eyes and shakes her arms in an agitated manner like a swallow about the take flight. Descending the stairs, she goes to the well, waters the flowers and, as the sweet perfume of the gillyflowers mixes with the harsh odor of euphorbia, the first stars rise over Monte.

Lia goes back to sit at the top of the stairs, with her hand on the rope, her eyes staring into the faint light.

That's how Noemi always remembered her, like she had seen her the last time as she passed her on the way to bed. They slept together in the same bed, but that evening she had waited in vain. She had gone to sleep waiting for her and she was still waiting....

The rest was confused in her memory: hours and days of mysterious anxiety and terror like one has with high fever. She saw again only Efix's livid, contracted face bent over almost as though searching for a lost object.

"Keep quiet, *padrone mie!*" he was murmuring, but then he had run through town asking everyone if they'd seen Lia, and he looked inside wells and far off into the distance.

Then Don Zame had returned....

At this memory a stormy rumble echoed in Noemi's mind. Each time it recurred she felt she had to move around, as though waking from a nightmare.

Then she got up and went to her room, the same room where she once slept with Lia. The same rusty iron bed with faded gold leaves, with bunches of grapes, only a few still slightly red and violet, like real unripe grapes; the same whitewashed walls, the small antique prints in black frames which no one in the house knew the value of; the same worm-eaten wardrobe whose decorative row of oranges and lemons glittered in the sunset like golden balls.

Noemi opened the wardrobe to put away her work, and the hinge creaked in the silence like a violin string, while the weak sun threw a faint rosy hue on the linens stacked on shelves lined with blue paper.

Everything was neatly in place. Up high some worn embroidery, silk rugs, wool blankets that long use had yellowed like saffron. Lower down, linens smelling of quince, and small asphodel and reed baskets with black paintings of vases, fish, little idols of primitive Sardinian art on a yellow background.

Noemi put her work inside one of these baskets and picked up another. Underneath it were family papers, records, legacies, proceedings of a lawsuit, tightly tied together with a yellow ribbon to ward off the evil eye. In addition to these dead papers, the yellow ribbon (which had not prevented their land from passing into other hands nor the lawsuit from being won by their adversaries) held a letter. Every time Noemi picked up the basket, she would look at it like someone on shore looks at a drowned body slowly jostled by the waves,

The letter was from Lia after she ran away.

Noemi was feeling something like memory sickness: her sisters' absence and an instinctive fear of solitude carried her back to the past. The same brilliant orange sunset, Monte covered with violet veils, evening smells – everything took her back to twenty years ago. Silent, black, in the faint light between the little window and the wardrobe, she herself seemed like a figure from the past, come from the ancient cemetery to visit the deserted house. She straightened the embroidery and the baskets and closed the door. The wardrobe door reopened with a squeal and seemed like the only living thing in the house.

Finally she made up her mind and removed the letter from the package of papers. It was still white, inside a white envelope, as though it had been written yesterday and no one had read it.

Noemi sat down on her bed, but she had just unfolded the letter and put a hand on the bronze ball when someone knocked on the door downstairs. First one knock, then three, then continuously.

With fear in her eyes, she looked down into the courtyard. It couldn't be the mailman. He's already come by....

The blows echoed in the silent courtyard. Her father used to knock that way when they were slow to open the door....

She dropped the letter and ran downstairs. But when she reached the door she stopped to listen. Her heart was pounding as though it had received the blows.

"Lord! Lord! It can't be...."

At last she asked hoarsely, "Who is it?"

"Friends," a strange voice replied.

But Noemi had trouble opening the door her hands were trembling so.

A tall, pale young man who looked like a laborer, dressed in green and wearing dusty yellow shoes and a little mustache the color of his shoes, stood in front of the door leaning against a bicycle. As soon as he saw Noemi he took off his cap that left its imprint on his thick golden hair, and smiled at her revealing nice teeth in full lips.

She recognized him immediately from his eyes – large, greenish-blue, almond-shaped eyes. They were Pintor eyes, but she grew even more perturbed when the stranger jumped up on the steps and embraced her tightly in his hard arms.

"Zia Ester! It's me.... And where are my other aunts?"

"I'm Noemi," she said, a little embarrassed, but she soon recovered. "We weren't expecting you. Ester and Ruth are at the festival."

"There's a festival?" he asked, holding his bicycle that had a dusty suitcase tied to it. "Oh, yes, I remember: the Feast of the Rimedio. Oh, there it is...."

He seemed to recognize the place where he was. There was the door his mother had talked about so many times. He began to untie his suitcase, flipping it with a handkerchief to remove the dust.

Noemi was thinking: "I have to call Zia Pottoi, I must send for Efix.... What can I do by myself? Oh, they left me here all alone when they knew he was coming...."

The embrace of that stranger, arriving from who knows where, from the streets of the world, inspired a vague fear; but she knew the rules of hospitality and didn't want to neglect them.

"Come in. Do you want to wash up? We'll take your suitcase upstairs. I'll call the woman who works for us.... I'm alone in the house right now... and I wasn't expecting you...."

She did her best to conceal their poverty; but it seemed he understood this too, because without waiting to be helped, after carrying the suitcase into the room that Zia Ester had prepared for him – the old guest room by the balcony – he came back down and went casually to wash at the well like the servant.

Noemi followed him with a towel over her arm.

"Yes, I've come from Terranova. What a road! You fly! Yes, I must have passed by the church, but I didn't notice anything. Yes, the town seems deserted. It's very dilapidated, yes...."

He answered yes to all Noemi's questions, but looked very distracted.

"Why didn't I write? After Zia Ester's letter I wasn't sure. Then I got sick and.... I don't know.... To tell the truth I just decided the day before yesterday. A friend was leaving. Then, yesterday, seeing the sea was calm, I left...."

As he dried his hands he headed toward the kitchen. Noemi followed him.

"Ester had written him! And he left just like that, like going to the festival!"

He sat on the ancient bench, facing Monte that threw its violet shadow in the kitchen, and crossed his long legs, folded his long arms across his chest and patted himself with his white hands. Noemi noticed that his socks were green, really a strange color for a man's socks, and she lit the fire, repeating to herself:

"Oh, so Ester had written to him in secret? Let her take care of him now!"

And she was almost afraid to turn and look at that figure of a man, a little strange all over, green and yellow, sitting motionlessly on the bench from which it seemed he would never rise again.

However, he began speaking about his trip, about the solitary road, and asked how long it took to go to Nuoro. He wanted to go to Nuoro: an administrator of a steam mill was there, a friend of his father's who had promised him a job.

Noemi looked up smiling happily. "How long? I don't know on a bicycle. A few hours. I went to Nuoro many years ago by horseback. The road is pretty, and the town is pretty, yes; the air is good, the people are good. They don't have the fever like we do here, and everyone can work and make money. All the foreigners have become rich over there, while this place seems dead...."

"Yes, yes, that's true!"

She went to get eggs to make an omelet.

"You know, you can't buy meat here every day. You can't find wine any more.... And this administrator of the mill, what's his name? Do you know him?"

No, he didn't know him, but he was certain that if he went to Nuoro he would get a job.

Noemi smiled with bitter irony, bent over her cooking. It was a bit early to say he'd find a job! A lot of people were looking for work! "You left the job you had?"

Giacinto didn't reply immediately; he seemed very preoccupied about the outcome of the omelet that she was cautiously turning.

Some drops of oil fell on the coals, filling the kitchen with fat smoke. Then the pan went back to frying quietly and Giacinto said: "It was a miserable job! And not very secure.... With too much responsibility!...."

He said nothing more, and Noemi asked no more. The hope that he would go to Nuoro soon made her good and patient. She set the table in the dining room, deserted and damp like a cellar, and began to serve him, apologizing that she couldn't offer him more.

"In this town we have to make do...."

Giacinto cracked nuts with his strong hands, listening to the tinkling of the flocks passing behind the house. It was almost night. Monte had grown dark and inside that damp room with green-stained walls he seemed to be in a cave, far from the world. Noemi's descriptions of the festival interested him. A little tired and sleepy, he looked at her, and that black figure outlined against the faint light in the window, with thick hair and little hands resting on the worn table, must have reminded him of his mother's stories, because he began to ask about villagers who were dead or in whom Noemi had no interest at all.

"Zio Pietro? What's this Zio Pietro like? He's the richest one, isn't he? How much does he own?"

"Yes, certainly he's rich. But he has a big head! Proud as a Jew."

"He loans money with usury?"

Noemi blushed, because even though relations with her cousin were tense, it seemed a personal injury to call a noble Pintor a usurer.

"Who told you that? Oh, don't say it even as a joke."

"But the Rector and his sister are usurers for sure. Are they rich? How much do they have?"

"No, not even them, what are you saying? Maybe, just maybe, Milese, but a fair usurer. Thirty percent, no more."

"Is this fair usury? What's unfair, then?"

Noemi bowed over the table and murmured: "Even a thousand percent.... Even more, sometimes."

Instead of showing surprise, Giacinto poured out a drink and said thoughtfully: "Yes, even for us the usurer's profit has become enormous.... Cardinal Rampolla's nephew was ruined that way!"

After supper he wanted to go out. He asked where the post office was, and Noemi took him as far as the street, pointing out the little square at the end of it, toward Milese's house.

As soon as he was out of sight she looked around and went down to Pottoi's place. Her door was open, but it was totally dark inside, and only after Noemi timidly called did the old woman come out of her hovel's dark depths with a burning stick in her hand. The rosy flame made her jewels glitter.

"Zia Pottoi, it's me! You have to send someone to get Efix right away. Giacinto is here. And then please come sleep with me. I'm afraid to be alone... with a stranger."

"I'll send someone to the farm. But I won't go to your house, no; I can't leave my house to the mercy of the sprite."

And to keep the sprite from entering during her absence, she left the burning stick on the door sill.

IV

A great mastic-wood fire, just like Noemi had seen as a girl, burned in the courtyard of Our Lady of Rimedio, illuminating the dark walls of the Sanctuary and the surrounding cabins.

A boy was playing the accordion, but those who had just come from the novena and were preparing supper or already eating inside the cabins were not ready to begin dancing yet.

It was still early: in the clear twilight the first stars were gleaming, and behind the high belvedere the rosy sky in the west was gradually fading.

A great peace reigned over the improvised village, and the accordion music and voices and laughter inside the cabins sounded far away.

Here and there black female figures bent over their sewing in front of little fires lit alongside the walls.

The men who came to the vigil to bring household items had already left with their carts and horses. Women, old men, children and some adolescents remained, and all of them, even though convinced they had come to do penitence, were trying to enjoy themselves as much as possible.

The two Pintor sisters had at their disposal two of the oldest cabins (every year new ones were built), appropriately called *sas muristenes de sas damas,* because they had almost become their private property after the gifts and donations their ancestors had made to the church from the time the archbishops of Pisa got off at the closest port on their pastoral visits to the Sardinian diocese and celebrated mass in the sanctuary.

Still there, between two cabins, in a corner of the courtyard, is the rock bench against the wall where Zia Pottoi had seen Donna Maria Cristina courted like a barona by all her subjects who had come in pilgrimage to the church.

Now Ester and Ruth were sitting there meek and black as two nuns with white kerchiefs, hands under their aprons, thinking about Noemi far away, about Giacinto far away.

Their supper had been frugal: a milk soup that didn't bloat the stomach and left their minds clear and pure as that great spring sky. And yet, from time to time, Ester felt something like a shudder of remorse, a secret, almost guilty, thought. Giacintino... the letter written in secret....

Next to them, sitting on the ground with her back to the wall, arms wrapped around her knees, Grixenda was laughing at the boy playing the accordion. In the adjacent cabin the relatives with whom she had come to the festival ate sitting on the ground around a *bertula* – or *bisaccia* – spread out like a table cloth, and while one of them cradled a sleeping baby and played with his hands, the other called to the girl.

"Grixenda, dear, come here and at least have a piece of cake. Do you want your grandmother to say we let you die of hunger?"

"Grixenda, don't you hear them calling you? Do what you're told," Ester said.

"Oh, Donna Ester! I'm not hungry.... I just want to dance!"

"Zuannantò! Come eat! Can't you see your music is like the wind? It blows people away."

"Wait until the leather wine bags are full and you'll see!" the usurer said, coming out from the little door to the right of the Pintor women, cleaning her teeth with a fingernail.

She too had finished eating and so as not to waste time set about spinning in the firelight.

Then the usual conversation began between her, the Pintor women, the girl and the other women inside. Just as in town they talked about the festival all year long, now at the festival they talked about the town.

"I don't know how you could have left your house unprotected, Comare Kallì. How could you?" said a tall girl who carried a jar of curdled milk under her apron, a gift from the priest to the Pintor sisters.

"Natolia, dear heart! I didn't leave treasures in my house like your master the Rector did!"

"Damn me! Well then, give me your key. I'll go rummage through your house, and then I'll run off to a big city!"

"Do you think a big city is a good place to be?" asked Ruth gravely, and Ester, who had emptied the jar of milk and given it back to Natolia with a tip inside, made the sign of the cross: "*Libera nos Domine.*"

Both were thinking about Lia's flight, about Giacinto's arrival, and they were surprised to hear Grixenda murmur: "But city folks want to come here!"

People started coming out into the courtyard. Women appeared at the doorways wiping their mouths on their aprons and ran after their children to get them to bed.

One of Grixenda's relatives went up to the accordion player and handed him a piece of bread.

"Eat it, sweetheart! What will your grandmother say? That I don't give you anything to eat?"

The boy stuck out his chin, tore off a bite and continued playing.

Irritated by the women's lack of interest in dancing, Grixenda and Natolia grew insolent.

"We know! You don't have fun if men aren't around!"

"Even Donna Ruth's servant Efix would do!"

"He's old as the hills! What would I do with Efix? Better to dance with a mastic stick!"

But suddenly, after barking from the belvedere, the priest's dog ran down to howl outside the courtyard, and the women quit their insults to go see who it was. Two men were coming up from the road, and while one of them looked like he was sitting on a little camel, the other looked like someone bent over a large grasshopper whose wings were sending the rider's long legs up and down. The firelight illuminated the mysterious figures as they approached. The first was Efix on a horse humpbacked with *bisacce* and pillows, the other a stranger whose bicycle shot red sparks across the courtyard.

Grixenda jumped to her feet and leaned against the wall in her excitement. Even the accordion player stopped.

"Donna Ester! Your nephew."

The trembling women stood up and Ester spoke in a tiny voice that resembled the bleat of a young goat.

"Giacintino!… Giacintino!… My nephew.… Am I seeing things or is it really you?…"

He dismounted and looked around in confusion. He felt his hands taken by the dry hands of his aunt, and he saw the pale face and pearl eyes of Grixenda against the black wall.

Then all the women crowded around him, looking, touching, asking questions. The warmth of their bodies seemed to bring him to life. He smiled and felt like he was in the middle of a large family, and began to embrace each one.

Some women jumped back, others began to laugh, looking up at him.

"Is that the custom in your town? He's confused us with Donna Ester and Donna Ruth! He thinks we're all his aunts!"

Efix picked up the pillows and carried them through the narrow little door into the empty cabin. Grixenda helped him spread them out on the wall bench, and it was she who swept out the little cell and made the little bed, listening to Giacintino's respectful and almost timid replies to his aunts' questions in the cabin next door.

"Yes, ma'am, from Terranova by bicycle. How was it? Like flying! On a road that flat and empty you could go around the world in a day! Yes, Zia Noemi was surprised to see me. She certainly wasn't expecting me, and she probably thought I'd come to the wrong door!"

His every word and strange accent struck Grixenda deeply. She hadn't clearly seen the face of the young man coming from far away places, but she had noticed his height and his thick golden hair like fire. And she already felt jealous because Natolia, the priest's servant, was hanging around in the women's cabin talking with him.

That Natolia was shameless! To please the stranger she was even making fun of the cabins, which after all were sacred because they were inhabited by the faithful and belonged to the church.

"Even Rome doesn't have palaces like these! Look at the curtains! The spiders made them for nothing, for the love of God."

"And can you count the mice? If you feel something scratch your feet tonight, don't think it's me, Giacì!"

Grixenda bit her lip and knocked on the wall to make Natolia shut up.

"There are ghosts, too. Hear them?"

"Oh, it's a woman knocking," Ruth said simply.

"Ghosts, mice, women are all the same to me," Giacinto replied calmly.

And Grixenda, leaning against the other side of the wall, began to laugh loudly. She listened to the young man's voice just as she had listened to the sound of the accordion a little earlier, and she laughed with pleasure; and yet, she felt like crying.

Everyone else was happy, but it was a grave happiness, in the women's poor cabin.

"It seems like a dream," Ester said, serving her nephew his dinner, while Ruth stared at him with her clear eyes. Efix bent over to take a bottle of wine from his *bisaccia*, and from that position he turned to smile at his mistresses.

Giacinto ate sitting on the wall bench that was used as a table and as a bed. And he too thought he was dreaming.

After Noemi's cold reception he had felt what he really was, a stranger among people different from himself; but now as watched his aunts serve him timidly, the servant smile at him like a baby, the girls look at him tenderly and boldly – he heard the sing-song of the accordion and saw shadows dance in the firelight – he imagined his life could always be like this, fantastic and happy.

"You have to adapt, "Efix said, pouring him something to drink." Look at water for example. Why do they say water's wise? Because it takes the shape of the vessel it's poured into."

"Wine, too, it seems to me!"

"Yes, wine, too! Only sometimes wine foams and moves; water never."

"Water, too, if you put it on the fire to boil," Natolia said.

Then Grixenda ran to the other side, took Natolia by the arm and dragged her away.

"Leave me alone! What's wrong with you?"

"You have no respect for the stranger!"

"Grixè! Has a tarantula bitten you that's made you crazy?"

"Yes, and because of that I want to dance."

Some women had already gathered around the accordion player, holding out their hands to begin the dance. The buttons on their bodices shone in the firelight, their shadows criss-crossed on the gray ground. Slowly they got in a line, with hands joined and feet raised to signal the first steps of the dance; but they were rigid and uncertain and seemed to lean on each other for support.

"It's obvious we need a leader! We need a man. Call Efix at least!" shouted Natolia, and as Grixenda pinched her arm, she added: "Oh, may a wasp sting you! You want me to be respectful to him, too?"

But Efix appeared and moved forward stamping his feet in cadence and waving his arms like a real dancer. He sang in accompaniment:

To the festa.... To the festa I've come....

Going up to Grixenda Efix took her arm, joined the line of dancers and the dance really did seem to come alive with his presence. The women's feet moved more agilely, coming together, sliding, lifting, their bodies became softer, their faces shown with joy.

"Here's the leader. Come on!"

"Up and away!"

A magic thread seemed to bind the women, giving them a quiet, glowing excitement. The thread began to bend, slowly forming a circle. From time to time a woman came forward, separated two joined hands, wove them into hers, and the black and red garland grew, behind which moved the fringe of shadows. Their feet moved more and more quickly, hitting one against the other, stamping the ground as though to wake it up.

"Up and away!"

Even the accordion sounded happier and livelier. Shouts of nearly wild joy echoed, as though demanding the dance to become more animated and voluptuous.

"*Uhi! Ahiahi!*"

Everyone ran to watch, and there, in the corner at the end of the courtyard, Grixenda could distinguish Giacinto's golden head between his aunts' two white kerchiefs.

"Efix, make your God-child dance!" said Natolia.

"That one's a leader, yes!"

"Put him next to the church and he'll look like the bell tower."

"Shut up, Natolia, big mouth."

"Your eyes speak louder than my mouth, Grixè."

"Burn in hell!"

"Hush up, women, and dance."

To the festa...to the festa I've come.

"*Uhi!Ahiahi!...*"

The shout whinnied like a horse. Scalded by the pleasure of the dance, the women's legs moved more briskly against their dark skirts, their feet emerging from the undulating red hem

"Don Giacinto! Come here!"

"Come on! Come on!"

The women looked over at him and smiled, their teeth gleaming at the corner of their mouths.

He jumped up, as though escaping from the prison of the two old women. However, once in the middle of the courtyard, he stopped, unsure what to do. Then the women's circle opened, formed into a line again and went to meet the stranger as in a child's game. Then they encircled him, took him in, closed again.

Tall, different from the others, he seemed like a pearl in the dance ring between Grixenda and Natolia; and he felt Grixenda's little hand trembling inside his, while the hard, warm fingers of Natolia entwined strongly in his as though they were lovers.

Even the priest came out of his cabin and watched, calm and rosy like a bald baby. Then he went to sit next to the Pintor sisters.

"A handsome boy, your nephew, Donna Ruth!"

He took out a silver snuffbox, shook it, opened it and put it first into Ester's cupped hand, then Ruth's, and finally gave some to Kallina.

"A handsome boy, Donna Ester, but just wait."

He raised his cassock to put the snuffbox back into his pocket and folded his blue handkerchief, slapping it against his chest.

"Donna Ester, just wait. We danced, too, when we had wings on our feet. And now what's Your Ladyship doing?"

Ester cried with joy, but pretended to sneeze.

"Your tobacco's like pepper, Father Paskà!"

Efix was happiest of all. Stretched out on a pile of grass in one of the empty *muristenes,* he felt like he was still dancing and admiring Giacinto, smiling at him like the women were.

He remembered running to his mistresses' house to see Lia's son: what a moment! His joy had been so overpowering he couldn't remember what he had said or done. He only remembered the cold but flustered figure of Noemi telling him, as though in secret:

"Go on, go to the feast.... They're waiting for you."

And she had sent them away, her face brightening only in the act of dismissal as the large door closed behind them.

Passing below the farm they had stopped for a moment, and with the tenderness of a lover Efix had pointed out his hill, the slope where the reeds trembled rosy in the sunset, his hut crouching in the green waiting for him.

"I live there year round. And you'll come when there's fruit and vegetables to take to town.... But this horse of yours can't carry the *bisaccia*!" he added, closing his eyes against the gleam of the bicycle.

"I'm going to Nuoro!" Giacintino said, still looking the farm up and down like he was looking a person over.

"You'll come to the farm sometime! Before it gets too hot, and besides in the autumn it's nice in the shade up there! And at night? The moon keeps you company like a bride. And the watermelons in the garden seem like crystal bowling balls."

"Yes, I'll come sometime," Giacinto promised, jumping off the machine swift as a bird.

And it had been Giacinto, won over by his companion's description, to suggest visiting the farm.

Together they had gone to the little farm, leaving the horse free to strip branches from the hedge wall.

Efix showed his new young master the embankment he had constructed with prehistoric methods, and the youth marveled at the rocks accumulated by the little man, and then looked at him as though to better measure the magnificence of the construction.

"All by yourself? What strength! You must have been strong as a young man!"

Efix grew red. "Yes, I was strong! And the path, didn't I make that?"

The path snaked upward, also reinforced by little stone walls, just as the various levels and knolls of the farm were sustained. A patient and solid work resembling that of the ancient builders of the stone *nuraghes.*

And at every terrace they stopped and turned to contemplate the little man's work, and the stranger's childish curiosity amused the servant.

"Does the river rise in the winter?... What's this?" he asked, pulling at a branch of a small tree.

He knew nothing about trees or herbs; he didn't know that rivers overran their banks in the spring! Here a row of chickpeas, already pale inside their pointed pods. There heavy tomato plants along the damp furrow, over there a little field of what looked like narcissus but was potatoes; onions trembling in the breeze like asphodels; cabbages plowed by luminous green caterpillars. Clouds of white and yellow butterflies flitted about, mingling with the pea blossoms. Grasshoppers leaped and fell as though flung by the wind, bees buzzed around the low wall, gilded by pollen. A row of poppies burned in the monotonous green of the bean field.

A solemn, fragrant silence descended with the shadows, and everything was hot and oblivious in that corner of the world enclosed by a wall of prickly pears, so much so that the stranger threw himself on the grass in front of the hut and didn't feel like going on.

May clouds passed by white and delicate as a woman's veils. Giacinto looked at the sky of overwhelming blue and felt like he had stretched out on a beautiful bed covered with silk.

He saw Efix open the hut, turn and beckon him with a mischievous gesture of his index finger; then he came back with something hidden behind his back and winked as he kneeled down. Was it all a dream?

Sitting up Giacinto hugged his knees and said a little prayer before taking the decorated gourd full of yellow wine the servant was holding out to him. Finally he drank: it was a sweet, fragrant wine like amber and to drink it like that, with his mouth on the gourd, gave him almost a voluptuous feeling.

Efix watched him, kneeling as though in adoration. He drank also and felt like crying.

Bees lighted on the gourd. Giacinto broke off a piece of grass, and looking at the ground, he asked: "How do my aunts live?"

The moment for confidences had come. Efix waved the gourd to the right and left.

"Look, as far as the eye can see in the valley was your family's. They were strong people! Now all that's left is this little farm, but it's like the heart that beats in the chest of old folks. They live on this."

"But how stubborn my grandfather was! He ruined the family...."

"If it weren't for him you wouldn't have been born!"

Giacinto raised his eyes and quickly lowered them again; they were full of desperation.

"Why be born?"

"Oh, what a fine question; because it's God's will!"

Giacinto didn't reply. He kept looking at the ground blinking his eyes, about to cry. Resigned, he closed his eyes and took another drink, while Efix sat down, crossed his legs and took one foot in his hand.

"Aren't you glad you came, Don Giacintì?"

"Don't call me 'Don,'" the youth said. "I'm not noble. I don't know anything! Talk to me like I talk to you. Am I glad? No. I came here because I didn't know where else to go.... Too many people where I come from.... And you have to be bad to make your fortune. You wouldn't know! There are lots of rich people.... But too many of them...."

He waved a finger toward the distance, as though pointing out a crowd of people, and Efix looked at his foot and murmured with tenderness and pity: "My poor boy!"

He would have liked to bend over the desolate "boy" and say to him: I'm here, you'll have everything you need! – but he didn't know what to do except offer him the gourd again like a mother offers her breast to her complaining baby.

"Of course we know what a devilish world that is! But it's different here. You can make your fortune. I'll tell you how

Milese did it.... One day he arrived like a bird without a nest...."

But Giacinto felt disconsolate as he listened, head down, his lips curling slightly with disgust. Suddenly he leaned an elbow on the grass, supporting his head in his hand, angrily chewing the sprig of grass.

"If you only knew! But what can you know? A prince in Rome owns more land than all of Sardinia, and another man who became great on his own donates more money than the king when there's some national disaster."

"In Sardinia there's a priest who has an income of three hundred scudi a day," Efix said, humiliated, but then he raised his voice: "I said three hundred scudi. Do you understand, Your Lordship?"

His Lordship did not seem surprised. But after a moment he asked: "Where is he? Can I meet him?"

"He's in Calangianus, in Gallura."

Too far away. And Giacinto, looking distracted, again took up his narration about the fabulous riches of the *Signori* of the "Continent," about their vices and dissipations.

"And are they happy?" asked Efix, beginning to be irritated.

"Are we happy?"

"Me, yes! Drink, drink and be strong!"

Giacinto drank and Efix shook the last drops on the grass. Bees lighted there and everything around was a buzzing sweetness.

However, after they went to the Church of the Rimedio, the boy seemed happy.

He had embraced his aunts and the other women, had eaten well and danced like a shepherd at the feast. Now he was snoring. A bit earlier Efix had looked at him sleeping next to the wall, his closed eyelids so delicate that the blue of his eyes seemed to show through, his reddish hair against the white of the pillow, fists closed like a dreaming baby. He had forgotten the burning lantern on the ground. Efix bent over to put it out, thinking that the Pintors were all like that: indifferent to economy and danger!

Oh, well, maybe that's better in life! He too lay down and closed his fists. Through holes in the roof stars pulsated and their twinkling and the incessant buzzing of crickets seemed in harmony.

He smelled alders and mint. Everything had fallen into a quivering silence as into running water. Efix remembered evenings long ago, the dance, the songs, Donna Lia sitting on a stone in the corner of the courtyard, bent over herself like a young prisoner gnawing her bonds and slowly preparing her escape.

V

The next morning at dawn Efix brought the horse back to town and told his young mistress about the pleasure of the previous evening. Noemi seemed calm, except that when he left for the farm she ran to the front door to remind him to go back in three days to deliver provisions to her sisters.

Three days later Efix returned. In order not to have to rent a horse, he slung his *bisaccia* over his shoulders and set off by foot.

The weather had cooled off: from the Nuorese mountains came a forest breeze that passed along the river as though wanting to go down to the sea with it.

Efix stopped near the alder tree at the sandy edge of the watermelon patch, and looking at the fleshy stems entangled like snakes under the leaves, he thought there was something almost alive, almost animal about them, like all the quivering bushes around them. And he spoke to them as though they understood, telling them not to break, not to dry up, to grow well and yield much fruit as was their duty; but a noise on the road distracted him.

Don Predu, proud and heavy on his fat black horse, was passing behind the hedge. He did an unusual thing when he saw Efix: he stopped.

"And what are we doing with this *bisaccia*? Have you been stealing beans?"

Efix stood up respectfully. "These are provisions for my mistresses. Where are you going?"

Don Predu was also going to the festa. The smell of the *gattò* cake he was taking to his friend the Rector came from his flower embroidered *bisaccia*, and the violet neck of a demijohn of wine protruded from it.

"Are you going on foot, you old fool? Are they making you be the horse now? Give me the *bisaccia*. I'll carry it for you. No, I won't run away! If you want to be sure, climb up on the haunches yourself, you old fool!"

Bewildered, after letting himself be urged and threatened a little, Efix loaded the *bisaccia* on the horse that seemed to sleeping. Then he climbed on behind Don Predu, trying to make himself as light as possible.

"Now your horse will get up a good sweat!"

"This horse, the devil help me, is the strongest in the district. You could load a mountain on it and he'd carry it. Look, he goes like he didn't even have a saddle. And tell me, what has that vagabond nephew of mine come to mess around in?"

Efix grimaced behind his back. Oh, that's why he's taking me!

"Why, vagabond? He was employed."

"What did he do? Count the hours?"

"A good job! In Customs. But, certainly, to live in those places you need a lot of money. One gentlemen there has as much land as Sardinia and another one gives more charity than the king."

Don Predu swelled with laughter. A silent, ferocious laughter.

"Oh, the boy's a windbag like you!"

"Why do you talk like that, Don Predu?" Efix said with dignity. "The boy's honest and good, without any vices. He doesn't smoke or drink, doesn't run after women. He'll make his fortune. If he wants, he can get a job right away in Nuoro. He even has money in the Bank."

"Have you counted it, you fool? Oh, Efix, 'pon my word, they give you stories to eat instead of bread. Tell me, how much do your noble *padrone* owe you?"

"They owe me nothing. I owe them everything."

"Quiet. If you're not I'll chuck you in the river. Listen, now you'll go even further in debt keeping that boy. You'll get money from Kallina, devil take you. You'll sell the farm. Remember I want it. If you don't tell me in time, if you do like you did other times, instead of selling to me for a good price you sold to others for half the price, watch out. I warn you, Efisè, I'll cut your throat. You've been warned."

The man behind him was panting, oppressed by a weight much heavier than the *bisaccia* that Don Predu had wanted to free him from.

"Lord, God! Why talk like that, Don Predu? Like an enemy of your poor cousins?"

"To the devil with my cousins, those old windbags! They're the ones who have always treated me like an enemy. So be enemies. But remember, Efix: I want the farm."

The torment lasted the whole way, until Efix, more tired than if he had walked, slid off the horse and pulled down his *bisaccia*.

Entering the churchyard he was greeted by the usual scene: his mistresses sitting on the bench with their hands on their laps, Kallina weaving, her stockingless feet in cloth slippers. Inside the cabins women sat on the floor drinking coffee, rocking babies, and high on the belvedere, against the golden sky, the black figure of Father Paskale waving his blue handkerchief.

"Are you enjoying yourselves?" Efix asked, laying the *biscaccia* at his *padrone*'s feet. "And him?"

"Always dancing," said Ester, and Ruth got up to put the food away.

The usurer spoke excitedly about Giacinto.

"What a pleasant boy! Doesn't talk much, but good as honey. Enjoys himself like a boy and comes here to eat my barley bread. Here he comes now from the fountain with Grixenda."

In fact, they could be seen in the distance, in the green of the scrub: he tall and greenish, she small and dark, with shining buckets in their hands that touched from time to time, and when the water overflowed the drops mixed with each other. The two of them seemed to enjoy that contact because they looked at the buckets and laughed.

Efix had a premonition. He went up to the priest and gave him a basket of cookies, a gift from a townswoman. From up there he saw Don Predu, who was at the fountain to let the horse drink, join Giacinto and Grixenda, and bend over to tell them something. All three laughed, the girl with her head down, Giacinto touching the horse's neck.

"Efix," said the priest, slapping his handkerchief on his chest to shake out the tobacco, "there's Don Predu. Good, we'll have a little gossip. Your Giacinto is a good boy; he goes to mass and the novena. Well mannered, pleasant. But take my advice and be careful!"

The priest's servants ran outside to help Don Predu unload his *bisacce*, while pale-faced women stood in the doorways, and after a little yipping, a dog jumped high in front of the horse almost as though to kiss it.

"Careful, women!" said Don Predu. "Something inside the *bisacce* will break if you touch it, just like you...."

"Go to the devil, Don Predu!" swore Natolia, yet looking at him languidly, trying to tempt him. Oh, if only she could! Then she would have revenge on Grixenda who had taken the stranger all for herself.

Grixenda also seemed excited by Don Predu's arrival.

"Look at that man," she said softly to Giacinto as they crossed the courtyard. "Your uncle's a man who enjoys himself and spends money at the feasts. He's not a spoil sport like you! If he has a hundred lire, he throws a hundred away, just like that!"

She dipped her fingers in the water and flipped it on his continually smiling face with sweet, desirous eyes, showing her his white teeth between red lips, almost as if he wanted to bite her.

"What's a hundred lire? I've spent a thousand in one night and didn't have a good time."

Grixenda put the bucket on a chair, and threw herself down beside a baby that smiled up at her from the pallet, waving his legs in the air, trying to grab her with his dirty hands. She kissed his legs, sinking her lips into the tender flesh with little rosy and violet-stripped furrows. She lifted him high and lowered him to the ground and lifted him again to make him laugh. Hugging him close to her breast she took him outside.

Giacinto was sitting down, dangling his hands between his knees, listening to Kallina who had invited him to eat some beans cooked in milk with her. They were speaking quietly, as though about serious matters, but Donna Ruth came to the door with a lamb's thigh, white with fat, with violet kidneys covered by a veil, and interrupted the conversation.

"Call Efix to make a wooden spit, Giacinto. Go!"

Grixenda herself ran to call the servant. She rubbed up against him like a cat and gave him the baby to kiss.

"I'm so happy, Zio Efix! Tonight we'll dance again! But look at your little gentleman. He seems to be courting Kallina!"

Efix looked at her tenderly; he saw Giacinto look up with eyes full of love and desire, and in his heart he blessed the two young people. Yes, enjoy yourselves, love each other. That's why we go to the festa, and the festa soon passes....

Sitting in the shade of the wall he began to whittle the spit. Women around him were laughing. As always, Giacinto was silent and seemed attentive to the sound of the accordion filling the courtyard with moans and shouts. But Natolia came up, swinging her hips.

"Father Paskà and Don Predu sent me to invite Don Giacinto to dinner."

After carefully brushing off his trousers, Giacinto stood up. Ester followed him with her eyes and looked a long time at the belvedere, as though fascinated by the sparkling glasses and silver tray that Natolia was waving around like a mirror. The idea that her rich cousin would notice the poor boy was enough to make her happy.

The women praised Giacinto, and the usurer, drawing a thread between her thumb and first finger and turning the spindle on her knee said with unusual sweetness: "I've never known such a nice boy. And handsome, too! He resembles the old Baron...."

"Who? The dead Baron who still lives in the castle?"

Ruth put her finger to her mouth. You mustn't speak of death at the festa.

"He's anything but a spirit. He's alive and has hands that move, isn't that right, Grixè? Who? Don Giacintino!"

But Grixenda leaning against the wall, the baby chewing the buttons of her blouse, was also looking at the gleaming tray on the belvedere, and her eyes seemed fascinated like those of her old grandmother who watched elves walking down by the river on moonlit nights.

Efix came again three days later. This time he was not alone. Almost everyone from town had come down for the festival, and the women carried on their heads trays with cakes and baskets full of chickens tied with red ribbons.

The little trees in the countryside were heavy with unripe fruit and the festival seemed to spread through the whole valley.

When Efix arrived he found the grounds already cluttered with carts, tents fashioned out of sacks and sheets, and in the shade of the church vendors of sweets and wine were behind their little stands.

A line of beggars waited on the path, their bent forms sallow and bluish, some with horrible white eyes, others with red wounds and violet tumors, with bare, thin chests, blackish arms and fingers groping like burnt branches. Between one bush and another they stood in profile against the bluish-white horizon. But beyond them green expanses and groups of horses with ponies gave a greater grandeur to the landscape.

Accordion music filled the air. The leaping and voluptuous motif was a call to dance, but at times it changed to a lament, as though tired of joy, as though regretting fleeting pleasures and complaining about the uselessness of everything. Then even the mares' melancholy eyes seemed full of sweet yearning.

Efix stopped a moment before a group from Nuoro. The women sat in a row in front of their cabins, waiting for the hour of the sung mass, and their scarlet bodices tinted the shadow of the wall red.

But mass was late. On the belvedere the priests were laughing and Natolia's sparkling tray passed back and forth among the dark figures.

Efix found the cabin deserted. His mistresses were in church and he went looking for them but was pulled aside by Don Predu, Milese, and Giacinto, standing in front of a wine booth, and three yellow glasses were stuck in his face.

"Drink, old fellow!"

"It's too early for me."

"It's never too early for a healthy man. Or are you sick?"

Don Predu pounded Efix hard on the back, thrusting him forward, sloshing wine on him. All for the love of God! He brushed off his clothes with his hands and drank. To his surprise and satisfaction he saw Giacinto pull out his wallet and hand the wine seller a fifty lira bill. God be praised, it means the boy really has money.

Besides, it was a day for joy. A quiet and almost melancholy joy for the women, toward whom the men, noisily enjoying themselves, showed a certain indifference.

All day long the accordion played, accompanied by the vendor's cries, the *morra* players' shouts – as they betted on their game – the choral singing, the improvised poetry.

Gathered inside one of the huts, sitting cross-legged on the floor around a demijohn which they faced like an idol, the poets improvised octaves for and against the war in Libya. There were many competing, and they went in turn, the other men and boys crowding around them. From time to time someone would bend over to pick up a glass of wine off the floor.

"Drink, devil!"

"To your health!"

"May we come to this festa for a hundred years, healthy and happy."

"Drink, devil!"

The poet Serafino Masala of Bultei, with a Greek profile and dressed like a Homeric hero, sang:

The Turk won't surrender,
He's anxious to fight.
The fierce Arab is courageous,
Ready to attack; he won't run....

Glasses passed from hand to hand; some women came timidly to the door.

Gregorio Giordano of Dualchi, a handsome, ruddy young man dressed like a troubadour, smoothed his long hair with both hands, pulled it away from his collar, and sang nearly sobbing, like a hired mourner.

Enough, I can't tell any more.
I'll try to remember what I can;
May the Italians have victory with every step,
To conquer all of Africa.
Heavenly saints, help them return
Calm and strong;
Help them return –
With good memories and virtue
And good health – to their homes.

Applause and laughter; everyone laughed, but they were touched.

However, in the church shadows, Efix heard another group of townsmen talking about America and emigrants.

"America? Anyone who hasn't been there doesn't know what it is. At a distance it looks like a lamb ready for shearing. Go near it and it eats you like a dog."

"Yes, dear brothers, I went there with a half-full *bisaccia* and thought I'd bring it back overflowing; I brought it back empty!"

A tall, thin man from the district of Baronia, dark as an Arab, invited Efix to have a drink and told him stories about the war he just returned from.

"Yes," he said, looking at his hands." I tore the hair off a *Sirdusso,* one of those devil worshipers. I made a vow to take it, the hair; to take it all off, skin and all. And so I did, strike me blind if I'm lying! I took it to my captain, holding it like a bunch of grapes; dark red blood was dripping from it like dark red grapes. The captain said: that's good, Conzinu!

Efix listened, holding a little red wild flower in his hand that he made the sign of the cross with, and said: "You must confess, Conzì. You've killed a man!"

"It's not a sin in war. As though it was done in secret? No!"

Then they began to argue. Efix looked at the little flower as though talking just to it.

But he had to interrupt the argument when Donna Ester motioned him over. It was time to eat. The priest had invited Giacinto, and everyone was eating what they had in good company. Clouds of good-smelling smoke issued from the cabins.

The sisters' corner was the quietest. Sitting in their cabin they ate roast lamb with Efix and talked about Noemi at home and Giacinto, about the priest and Milese, smiling kindly.

"At first," Ruth said as she cut a little cake into three equal portions, "Giacinto talked about going to Nuoro, where he said he had work in the mill. Now he hasn't mentioned it for two days."

"We haven't seen him for nearly two days; he's always with Predu and the others."

"Let him enjoy himself," Efix said.

Kallina sat outside her door, lounging uncharacteristically on her rock, and Grixenda, pale and sad, stared at the priest's belvedere with the baby on her lap.

Ah, Giacinto was enjoying himself up there, forgetting about her. And she seemed to be crouching on the edge of a desert, in front of a mirage.

Efix came out and said to her: "Why aren't you enjoying yourself?"

She straightened the yellow ribbon on the baby's bonnet put there to ward away the evil eye, and her eyes filled with tears.

"Everything is over for me!"

Her relatives called her from the cabin: "Grixenda, come here! What will your grandmother say when she sees you so thin? That we don't give you anything to eat?"

"Ah, she just needs a bite," Kallina said to Efix, after calling him with a wink. "Come, Efix, drink a glass of vernaccia. Do you know who gave it to me? Your little *padroncino*. Good as bread, and pleasant. Listen, you've got to tell him that Grixenda's not for him!"

"Let them enjoy themselves. We're at the festa!"

"We come here to do penitence, not to sin. Yes, my relatives feed Grixenda, but they don't notice where she goes day and night with Don Giacinto."

"And my *padrone*? Don't they notice?"

"Them? They're like wooden saints in churches. They look but don't see. Evil doesn't exist for them."

"That's true!" Efix admitted. He drank, but felt sad and went to lie down under a mastic tree.

From there he saw the tall grass waving, almost following the monotonous drone of the accordion, and the horses standing in the sun like paintings against the enamel blue of the horizon.

Voices were lost in the silence, figures faded in the light. There a woman's shape appeared next to a bush, a man's shape joined hers, and they drew so close they formed a single shadow.

A shiver ran down Efix's spine, and yet, breaking off a daisy and chewing on the stem, he watched without envy as Grixenda and Giacinto embraced. God bless them and keep them always like this, in the sun and light.

In the early evening the festa became more animated. The men showed themselves more expansive with the women, dragging them to dance, and the oblique sun tinged the buzzing courtyard pink.

At sunset everyone gathered in the church and the many voices rose as one, blended together just as the bushes outside were blending their perfume. Kneeling in a corner, Efix felt his usual sorrowful ecstasy. Next to him Grixenda was kneeling stiff as a wooden angel and her singing was a moan of love.

The red twilight, defeated by the candlelight as it approached the altar, spread over the congregation like a veil of blood. Little by little the veil turned dark, barely brightened by the golden candlelight. The congregation didn't leave, and even though the priest had finished his orations it continued to intone the holy lauds. It was like the distant murmur of the sea, the forest rustling in evening. It was an ancient people marching on and on, singing the simple prayers of the early Christians, going down a gloomy road, enraptured with sorrow and hope, toward a place of light, but distant, unreachable.

With his head in his hands Efix sang and wept. Grixenda looked ahead with damp eyes reflecting the candle flame, and she too sang and wept. Their pain was mutual. And their pain together was the same as all those others there who like the servant remembered a past of shadows, and like the girl dreamed of a future of light. The pain of love.

Then all was silence.

Zuannantoni, impatient to take up his accordion again, was the first to leap up with his cap in his hand. At the door he stopped, looked out and gave a shout. Everyone ran outside to look. The new moon grazing the courtyard wall looked like it wanted to come in.

After supper they began to sing and shout around the fires. Even Don Predu danced, making all the women happy who hoped he would choose them.

Only Giacinto wasn't dancing, sitting next to the usurer, pale and tired, his hands dangling between his knees. Efix had heard the women arguing about who had spent more money that day and who had the most fun, and someone said it was Don Predu.

"No, it's Don Giacinto. He spent more than three hundred lire. But he's rich. They say he has a silver mine. How he's enjoyed himself!"

"He paid for everyone's drinks, even for people he didn't know."

"Why does he do that?"

"My goodness, because whoever has it spends it."

Efix felt satisfaction and apprehension at the same time. He sat down next to Giacinto and repeated the women's chatter.

"A silver mine? Yes, it produces, but not like an oil well. A woman I know dreamed that there was oil in a certain place, on a gentleman's land who had fallen on bad times. He was so desperate he was ready to kill himself. He drilled in the place that women dreamed about and now he's so rich he can give her twenty thousand lira a month."

"Why didn't he marry the woman who had the dream? Or did she already have a husband?" Efix asked thoughtfully.

The women were dancing. Grixenda, with her burning face was laughing like she was the happiest one there. Efix touched Giacinto's knee and murmured: "They say...look at that girl.... She's good, but poor. An orphan...."

"I'll marry her," Giacinto said, but he was looking at the ground and seemed to be dreaming.

VI

During times of famine, that is, the weeks before the barley harvest, when people run out of grain and turn to the usurer, old Pottoi went fishing for blood suckers. Her favorite spot was a bend in the river below Dove's Hill near the Pintor women's farm.

She would sit there for hours, in the shade of the alder tree, her bare legs in the transparent greenish water flecked with gold. Keeping a bottle firm on the sand with one hand, she touched her necklace with the other.

From time to time she bent over and watched her feet undulating, large and yellowish in the water. She would draw out one leg, pull off a black shining berry, put it in the bottle, and push it down with a reed. The berry would stretch, shrink, take the shape of a black ring. It was a bloodsucker.

One day, toward the middle of June, she went up as far as Efix's hut. It was very hot and the yellow valley spread out below under a blue-veiled sky.

The servant was weaving a mat in the shade of the reeds with fingers trembling from malaria fever. When the old woman sat down at his feet with the bottle in her lap, he raised his slightly veiled eyes and waited, resigned, as though he already knew what she wanted from him.

"Efix, you're a God-fearing man. You can speak frankly with me. What are your young master's intentions? He comes to my house, sits down, says to the boy: play the accordion (he gave it to him). Then he says to me: I'll send Zia Ester to ask for Grixenda's hand. But Donna Ester hasn't come around, and the day I went there Donna Noemi heaped so much abuse on me I left more dead than alive. Then, when I got back home, even Gixenda was sassy because she didn't want me to go to your *padrone*. I don't know where to turn, Efix. We didn't ask him to come here. He came on his own. Kallina tells me to kick him out. But does she kick him out when he goes there?"

Efix smiled. "He certainly doesn't go courting there!"

The old woman looked up at him with irritation, and the thick cord-like muscles on her neck seemed to lengthen more than usual.

"And you think he comes courting to my house? No, he's an honest boy. He doesn't even touch Grixenda's hand. They love each other like good Christians waiting to get married. Tell me, in all honesty, Efix, what are his intentions? Do me this kindness, for your master's soul."

Efix became thoughtful. "Yes, one evening at the feast he told me he'll marry her.... Honestly, though, I don't think he can."

"Why? He's nobility."

"I'll say it again. He just can't, woman!" said Efix more strongly.

"He has money, I've seen it. He spends it like water. And I remember your dead master said, when he was young and came to my house and my grandmother was alive: love's what binds a man to a woman, and money binds a woman to a man."

"Him? He said such a thing? Who did he say that to?"

"To me, are you deaf? Yes, to me. I was fifteen years old and innocent. My grandmother chased Don Zame off and made me marry Priamu Piras. My Priamu was quite a man. He had a goad with an awl at the end that he'd put up to my eye and say: see? I'll poke your eye out if you look back at Don Zame when he looks at you. And so time went by. But the dead come back. When Don Giacintino sits on the stool and Grixenda in the doorway, it seems to be me and the blessed dead man...."

When she began to ramble like that Efix knew she'd never stop. He was getting irritated with her and sent her away.

"Go in peace! Look for a man with a good prod for your granddaughter!"

The old woman, happy to know that on one evening of the feast the boy had said "I'll marry her," went away without another word. Efix remained alone facing the red moon that was rising through the gray evening vapors, but he felt restless. In the drowsiness in which the whole valley was immersed, the murmur of the river seemed like the buzzing of fever, and the crickets' songs sounded like relentless complaining.

No, the life Giacinto was leading was not that of an honest, God-fearing young man. As the days went by the great hopes held for him were dashed, leaving a deep anxiety in their place. He spent money and wasn't earning any. Even the deepest well can run dry with too much use, Efix thought.

Some evenings Giacinto came to the farm to take fruit and vegetables back to town that his aunts then sold secretly out of their home like stolen goods, since it's not proper for noblewomen to be greengrocers. That was the most useful thing he did. The rest of the time he loafed around town. There he comes up the path dragging the dusty bike alongside him like a dog, panting as though coming from the ends of the earth. After tossing a parcel to the servant he threw himself on the ground like a dead man.

And he had the pale face and gray lips of a dead man; but a tremor shook his left shoulder so hard it frightened Efix. He pulled a glass tube from his pocket and dropped two quinine pills in the palm of his hand, which he then put in the boy's mouth.

"Swallow them. You have the fever!"

Giacinto swallowed the pills, and without sitting up he took his head in his hands.

"I'm so tired Efix! Yes, I have the fever. I've really got it! How can anyone not get it in this damned town? What a town!" he added tiredly, as though talking to himself. "I'm dying, I'm dying...."

"Get up," Efix said, bending over him. "Don't stay there. The evening air's bad for you."

"Let me die, Efix! Leave me alone! It's so hot! I've never been so hot. At least there we could go swimming."

What could Efix say to comfort him? "Why didn't you *stay* there?" Efix felt too much pity for the misery lying prostrate before him to say that.

"What did you do today?" he asked quietly.

"What do you think I did? There's nothing to do! Come here to bring you bread, go back there with things from the garden! And *those* three who live like mummies! Zia Noemi's a little upset today because Zia Ester told me they didn't have money for taxes. Of course, they spend money on me and don't want anything back! I told Zia Ester: don't worry, I'll go to the tax office. Zia Noemi's a fury! She has eyes like a mad cat. I couldn't believe how quick tempered she is. And then she said to me: with your money, if you have any, you can buy another accordion, one for Grixenda. What's so bad about me going to see her, Efix? Where else can I go? Zio Pietro takes me to the tavern, and you know I don't like wine; Milese wants me to gamble (that's how he made his fortune!) and I don't like to do that. I go see that girl because she's good, and the old woman says funny things. What's bad about that? Tell me, tell me."

Giacinto looked up at him imploringly, his sweet eyes reflecting the moon. Efix opened the package of bread but couldn't eat; deep anguish restricted his throat.

"Nothing bad! But even though the girl's good she's poor and not worthy of you."

"Love doesn't care about poverty or nobility. How many *signori* have married poor girls. You don't know anything about it. More than one English lord, more than one American millionaire has married servants, teachers, singers…why? Because they loved them. And they're rich. They're kings of oil, copper, tin! Who am I compared to them? And the women? Russian princesses, Americans, who do they marry? Don't they fall in love with poor artists and even with their coachmen and servants? But what could you know about it?"

Efix squeezed a piece of bread in his hands and his tormented heart felt squeezed by memories.

"And then they say they believe in God! Why don't they let me marry the woman I love?"

"Be quiet, Giacinto! Don't talk about them like that! They want what's good for you."

"Then they should let me have my own family. I'd even bring Grixenda into their house to help them. They're old now. I'll work. I'll go to Nuoro, I'll buy cheese, livestock, wool, wine – yes, even wood, because now with the war on everything is valuable. I'll go to Rome and offer the goods to the Minister of War. You know how much money there is to make?"

"Who knows! And the capital?"

"Don't worry, I have it. Just let *them* leave me in peace. I didn't come to take advantage of them or to live off their backs. Oh, Zia Noemi is awful!" he suddenly began shaking, hiding his face in his hands. "Oh, Efix, I'm so unhappy! Besides, I'm ashamed to see them living in such poverty, secretly selling potatoes, pears, and apples to children who come sneaking into their courtyard with coins in their fists, asking for the stuff under their breath almost as if the things were stolen! Yes, it makes me ashamed! This has to stop. They could go back to being what they were, if they would leave it to me. If Zia Noemi knew what I wanted to do for them she wouldn't act that way."

Efix was touched. "Giacinto! Give me your hand. You're a good boy!"

They were silent. Then Giacinto began to speak again in a sweet, gentle voice that vibrated like a child's in the lunar silence.

"Efix, you're a good man. I want to tell you something that happened to a friend of mine. He worked with me at the Customs Office. One day a rich retired port captain, a big good man but naive as a baby, came to make a payment. My friend said: Leave the money and come back later for the receipt that has to be signed by my superior. The captain left the money. My friend took it, left, gambled it and lost. When the captain returned, my friend denied receiving the money!

The man protested and went to the superiors, but since he didn't have a receipt everyone laughed in his face. Still, my friend lost his job...yes, that would be four months ago...yes, I remember, it was during carnival time. He went dancing. He drowned his problems in drink until he didn't have a coin left. He left the dance with pneumonia and fell on a street bench. They took him to the hospital. When he came out, all weak and exhausted, he didn't have a home, he didn't have anything to eat. He slept under the arches of the port, he coughed and had bad dreams. He always dreamed the captain was following him...like a scene in a movie. And then one evening the captain really did come looking for him under the arches. My friend thought he was still dreaming, but the man said to him: 'I've been looking for you for quite a while. I know its too late to do anything about the money, but I want your superiors and everyone to know the truth. It'll be better for you, too. Tell me honestly, did you spend the money or not?' My friend answered yes. Then the captain said: 'Let's try to straighten things out. I don't want to ruin you. Here's my address. Come to my house tomorrow and we'll go to your superiors together.' Fine! But the next day my friend didn't go. He was afraid. So afraid. And besides the weather was terrible and he couldn't move from there. He was coughing and a porter brought him some hot milk from time to time. What weather! What weather!" Giacinto repeated, and looked around almost to assure himself that the night was mild.

Efix listened with his elbow on his knee, his face in his hand, like children listen intently to fairy tales.

"But one day I made up my mind and went...."

Silence. The faces of the two men grew dark and they lowered their eyes. Giacinto trembled convulsively, but then sat up and shook himself as though to free himself from trembling. He went on in a harsher tone:

"Yes, it was me, you already knew that. I went to the captain. He wasn't home, but the maid, a pale girl who spoke quietly, had me wait in an antechamber. The room was almost dark, but I remember that when a door opened the red floor shone like it was washed in blood. I waited hours. Finally the captain returned. He was with his wife, as big as he was, and as good natured. They seemed like two enormous children; they laughed loudly. The signora opened the door to get a better look at me. I coughed and yawned. They saw I was hungry and invited me to the dining room. I got up, I remember, and fell back hitting my head on the back of the settee. I don't remember anything else. When I woke up I was in a bed in their home. The maid brought me a cup of broth on a silver tray and spoke to me very respectfully. I stayed there more than a month, Efix, you understand: forty days. They made me well, they tried to get me a job, but work was hard to find because everyone knew my story by now. Besides I wanted to go far away, over the sea. No one can know what I suffered during that time. I still see the captain, his wife, the servant, in dreams; I see them in reality, too, now in front of me. They were good, but I'd crawl in a hole not to see them any more. And the worst is that I *couldn't* leave their house. I stayed there, stupefied, sitting quietly listening to the signora who couldn't stop talking, or in the company of the servant who never said anything. I sat at their table, listening to them joke and make plans for me as though I were their son, and it all hurt me, humiliated me, even though I *couldn't* leave. Finally one day the signora saw I was completely well and asked me what I intended to do. I said I wanted to come here to see my well-off aunts I had talked about. Then they bought me a ticket for the trip and even gave me a bicycle. I understood it was time to go, and so I came here. What a liberation at first! But now, in my aunts' house, it's like I'm still there.... I don't know...."

A somewhat mocking cry traversed the silence of the ridge above the two men. Giacinto jumped up in surprise, thinking that someone had been listening to his story and was laughing at him. But he saw a small long gray shape followed by another darker, shorter shape jump as though flying from one bush to another around the hut and disappear without even giving him time to pick up a rock to throw at them.

Efix was also on his feet. "They're foxes," he said quietly." Let them run. They're making love. At times they seem like elves," he continued while Giacinto threw himself silently on the ground once again. "Did you see how long they were? They're devils about eating the green grapes."

But Giacinto had grown silent. Efix didn't know what to say, whether to beg him to finish his story, or to comfort him, or to comment about what he had just heard, for the good or bad. That was why he had been sad all day long. That was the way life goes! But what to say? Deep down he was glad the foxes had made Giacinto stop talking. Nevertheless, something needed to be said.

"Well, then...that captain? It's obvious he was a wise man. He understood that youth...youth...is liable to make mistakes.... And then, when one is an orphan! Come on, get up. Do you want to eat?"

Efix went into the hut and came back pealing an onion. Giacinto was quiet, downcast, perhaps regretting his confession, and he didn't dare say another word.

The odor of the onion mixed with the sweet-smelling grass around them, with the vines and sarsaparilla. The foxes ran by again. Efix ate, but the bread tasted bitter. Two or three times he tried to say something, but he just couldn't. It all seemed like a dream. Finally he shook Giacinto, tried to lift him up, saying gently: "Come on inside! The fever's going around."

But the young man's body seemed made of bronze, stretched out heavily on the ground as though it would never rise again.

Efix went back into the hut, but put off closing his eyes, and even when asleep he had the painful thought that he should respond to Giacinto's story. But he didn't know what to say, good or bad.

"I should tell him: oh, well, cheer up. You'll make amends! After all you were just a boy, an orphan...."

He dreamed that Noemi looked at him with her evil eyes, and quietly said through her teeth: "See him? See what kind of man he is?"

He awoke with a heavy heart. Even though it was still night he got up, but Giacinto had already gone.

For many days Giacinto was nowhere to be seen, so Efix began to grow uneasy – also because the vegetables and apples were piling up in the shade of the hut and no one came to get them.

Every evening Don Predu, who owned large farms toward the sea, would pass by on his way back to town. If he saw the servant he would point a finger toward his cousins' land and then touch his chest to signify that he was waiting for the condemnation and dispossession in order to take over the farm; but accustomed to that reminder, Efix would salute him in turn and motion, no, no, with his hand and head.

After Giacinto's confession he felt uneasy when he saw Don Predu: he looked more mocking than usual.

One evening he waited for him next to the hedge, and said: "Don Predu, tell me, have you see my young master? The other evening he was here he had fever and now I'm worried about him."

From high in his saddle Don Predu laughed, with his forced, closed mouth, swollen cheek laugh.

"I saw him gambling last night with Milese. And he was losing, too!"

"He was losing!" Efix repeated, perplexed.

"What do you mean! Do you expect him always to win?"

"He told me he never gambled."

"And you believed him? He couldn't tell the truth if you shot him. But he's not bad. He tells lies because they seem like the truth to him, like little boys do."

"Like a little boy, certainly."

"But a little boy with all his teeth! And how he chews! He'll even eat up this farm. Efix, remember. I'm here. If you don't, I'll beat you...."

Efix looked up, frightened. In the red sunset the big man on the horse looked like a bird of ill omen, one of the many night monsters he feared.

"Jesus, save us. Our Lady of Rimedio remember us."

Don Predu was already on his way when Efix caught up with him on the big road. With both hands he held out a basket full of tomatoes and greens.

"Don Predu, have your servant take this to my *padrone*. I can't leave the farm...and Don Giacinto doesn't come...."

At first the man looked at him in surprise, then a kind smile rippled across his fleshy lips. He raised a leg and said: "Look, there's room."

Efix put his basket inside the *bisaccia* and returned to his hut while Don Predu rode away without another word. He was afraid his employers might scold him. He knew he had done something serious, perhaps made a mistake, but he wasn't sorry. A mysterious hand had pushed him, and he knew that all actions accomplished this way, by supernatural power, were good ones.

He waited for Giacinto until late that evening. A full moon whitewashed the valley, and the night was so clear that each blade of grass had a distinct shadow. The phantoms didn't dare come out it was so light. The murmur of the water was lonely when not accompanied by the *panas* beating their laundry. Even they were peaceful this night. Only the servant couldn't sleep. He was thinking of Giacinto's story about the port captain, and felt a sense of infinite sweetness, of infinite sadness.

We all sin, everyone in the world, sooner or later, more or less, and so? Hadn't the captain been forgiving? Why couldn't others forgive him? Oh, if we could all forgive each other! The world would have peace. Everything would be clear and tranquil, like on this moonlight night.

He got up to make the rounds of the farm. Yes, on the white path the shadow of flowers was drawn. Even the prickly pear thorns showed in its shadow, and down on the river, where the water was still, stars could be seen.

But wait, behind the hedge among the alder trees a shadow was moving. It was a black, deformed animal with silver legs. It creaked on the sand and then stopped.

Efix ran down. He seemed to be flying.

"It's you! Is it you? You frightened me."

Giacintino pulled his bicycle along at his side and followed him silently; but when he reached the hut he threw himself on the ground once again, moaning: "Efix, Efix, I can't take any more.... What you have done! What you have done!"

"What have I done?"

"I don't know myself. Zio Pietro's servant came bringing a basket, saying that you had given it to his master. Zia Ruth and Zia Noemi were in the house, and Zia Ester was at the novena. They took the basket and thanked the servant, and even gave her a tip, but then Zia Noemi had a fainting fit. Zia Ruth thought she was dead, and shouted. I ran to call Zia Ester; she came scared to death, and for the first time even she gave me a grim look and said I had come to kill them all. Oh God, God, oh God, God! I bathed Zia Noemi's face with vinegar and I was crying. I swear to you on my mother's grave I was crying without knowing why. Finally Zia Noemi came to and waved me away. She said she'd rather die than see this day. I asked her why. Why, Zia Noemi, why? And she waved me away with one hand and covered her eyes with the other. It's terrible! Why did I ever come, Efix? Why?"

The servant didn't know what to say. Now he could see he did wrong by giving the basket to Don Predu, and he was trying to think of a way to set it straight, but he didn't see how, he didn't know why, and once again he felt all the weight of the women's misfortunes.

"Calm down," he finally said. "I'll go to town tomorrow and straighten it all out."

That made Giacinto feel better. "You've got to tell them it wasn't my idea to give the basket to Zio Pietro. They think it was. They think – especially Zia Noemi – that I'm trying to make friends with Zio Pietro to spite them. I'm friends with everyone; why shouldn't I be with Zio Pietro? But my aunts know he wants to buy their farm. Is that my fault? Am I the one who wants to sell it?"

"No one wants to sell it. Why talk about it? But you, dear boy, you…you said a lot of things the other evening. You promised to move heaven and earth to make your aunts happy; and then last evening you went to play cards…."

"Sometimes you can make money playing cards. I want to make money just for *them*. No, I don't want to be a burden to them. I'd rather die." He added softly, "Look, now, after that scene today, I feel like I'm still in the captain's house…. God help me, Efix!"

Efix was listening with dread. Once again he was confronted by the tragic destiny of the family which he was stuck to like moss to a rock, and he didn't know what to say or what to do.

"Oh," Giacinto sighed deeply. "I'm going away from here for sure; I won't wait until they send me away! My aunts have no charity, especially Zia Noemi. But I don't care. She didn't forgive my mother; how could she forgive me? But I, I…."

He looked down and took a letter from his pocket.

"See, Efix? I know everything. If Zia Noemi didn't forgive my mother after this letter, how can she be good? You know what's in this letter. You brought it to Zia Noemi. I took it; it was on the bed the day I arrived. I read some of it, and then I took it out of the wardrobe today…. It's mine. It's from my mother. It belongs to me…. This letter doesn't belong here."

"Giacinto! Give it to me!" said Efix, holding out his hands. "It's not yours! Give it to me. I'll take it back to them."

But Giacinto held the letter tightly and shook his head. Efix tried to take it. He begged like he was begging for his life.

"Giacinto, give it to me. I'll take it back myself, I'll put it back in the wardrobe. I'll talk to them, I'll make peace. You wait for me here. But give me the letter."

Giacinto looked at him. His was shaking, but his eyes were cold, almost cruel. Then Efix jumped up, gripped his shoulders and whispered one word into his ear. "Thief!"

Giacinto felt he was being attacked by a vulture. He opened his hand and let the letter fall to the ground.

VII

At dawn Efix set off for the village.

Nightingales were singing, and the whole valley was golden – a bluish-gold reflected from the luminous sky. Some shapes of fishermen were as still as though painted against the green riverbank and the green of stagnant water over white stones.

Although it was early when he reached the village, Efix saw the usurer weaving in her courtyard, surrounded by fat little pigs and cooing doves, and he greeted her by motioning that he would come back later; she replied with a shake of the spindle. She could wait. She wasn't in a hurry.

Further up he saw Zia Pottoi with a cup of milk for the children's breakfast. Efix tried to keep on going, but the old woman began to talk loudly and he had to stop to listen to her.

"Well, now, what have I done? If children can love one other, why must we old people hate each other?"

"I'm in a hurry, Comare Pottoi."

"I know, there's something going on at your *padrone*'s house. But it's not my fault. I'm not to blame this time. Your young master wants Grixenda to stay home and not go barefoot, and not take in any more washing. I have to be a servant, but I do it gladly since it's a matter of keeping the children happy...."

"Lord, help us!" sighed Efix. "Let me go, Comare Pottoi. Pray to Christ, pray to Our Lady of the Rimedio."

"The remedy is in us," the old woman pronounced sententiously. "You need courage, nothing else."

"You need courage," Efix repeated to himself, as he approached the Pintor sister's house.

All was silence and sun in the courtyard: jasmine bloomed over the well and the bones shone in the golden grass of the ancient cemetery. Monte hovered over the house with its green-gold cape. One of the decorated columns had fallen from the balcony and lay on the pebbles like remains of a rocket. All was silence.

Efix entered the house and saw that the basket he had sent with Don Predu was nearly empty, a sign that the vegetables had already been sold: only the yellow apples were left. He felt like it had all been a dream. He sat down and asked: "Where are the others? What's happened?"

"Ester is at mass. Noemi is upstairs," Ruth said, bent over to prepare coffee.

She said nothing more until her sisters arrived: Ester with her fingers grasping her crossed shawl, Noemi pale and silent with her violet eyelids lowered.

Efix didn't dare look at them. He stood up respectfully while they took their places on the bench, and only after Ester had asked, "Efix, do you know what happened?" did he raise his eyes and see that Noemi was staring at him like a judge staring at the accused.

"I know. It's my fault. But I meant well."

"You always mean well! It would be nice if sometimes your intentions weren't quite so well meaning! But in the meantime...."

"After all he wasn't an enemy! He's a relative!"

"'Your own people, your misfortune,' Efix!"

"Well, then, don't do it again, you mean!"

"Has he gone?" Ester asked anxiously.

"Gone? Don Predu? Where?"

"Who's talking about Predu? I was talking about that shameful boy."

Efix looked at the basket. "I meant Don Predu...about what I did yesterday."

Noemi smiled, but a smile that twisted her mouth toward her left ear.

"Efix," she said crossly," we're talking about Giacinto. Before we decided to have him come, you said: 'If he behaves badly I'll send him away.' Did you or did you not say that?"

"That's what I said."

"Then keep your promise. Giacinto is the ruin of our family."

Efix lowered his head for a moment. He was blushing and ashamed of it, but he immediately recovered and asked: "May I say something? Something badly said is as though not said."

"Go ahead."

"The boy doesn't seem bad to me. He's been badly guided up to now. He lost his parents at the worst time for him, and he's been like a little boy alone in the street, and he lost his way. He has to be to lead back to the right way. Now, here in town he doesn't know what to do. He has the fever, he's bored, that's why he plays cards and goes courting. But he has a good head, he's well brought up. Has he ever been disrespectful?"

"No, not that...." broke out Ester, and even Ruth shook her head no. But Noemi said in a bitter voice, slowly tightening her fists and extending them toward Efix: "Ever since he arrived he's been nothing but disrespectful. Yes, he came without saying anything.... As soon as he came he made friends with everyone who disrespects us. Then he began courting a girl who belongs to the worst family in Galte. One who goes barefoot to the river! And he's been lazy, and lives with vice, you said it yourself. If this isn't lacking respect to us, to our house, what is? Tell me, in all good conscience...."

"It's true," admitted Efix. "But he's just a boy, like I said. We need to help him, to find him a job. Then I'd like to say something else...."

"Go ahead and say it!" Noemi said, but with such contempt that he froze. Nevertheless he took a chance: "I think he'd like to have a family of his own. If he really loves that girl...why not let him marry her?"

Noemi jumped up, leaning her trembling legs against the chair.

"Did he pay you to say that?"

Now he had the courage to look her in the eye, and the single reply, "I'm not accustomed to being paid," filled his mouth with bitter saliva. But he swallowed the words along with the saliva because he saw Ester pull on Noemi's jacket, and pale Ruth look at her pleadingly, and he understood that they had guessed his reply, and knew he wasn't a servant to be paid; or rather, yes, a servant, but a servant that no amount of money in the world could compensate.

"Donna Noemi! You say things before you think, Donna Noemi! Your nephew doesn't have the money to pay me, and even if he had it wouldn't be enough!" he said, shaking with bitterness, and Noemi sat down again, putting her hands on her knees as though to hide the trembling.

"As far as that goes he has money! Not his, but he has some."

"And who gives it to him?"

Six eyes stared at him in amazement. Noemi began to smirk, but Ester put a hand on hers and spoke sweetly. "He takes money from Kallina. We thought you knew that, Efix! He borrows money from Kallina, and Predu has signed some notes because he hopes to get the farm out of it. Understand!"

He understood. With head bowed, eyes closed, livid, he opened and closed his fists in fear and was unable to speak.

"And you thought I knew? How? ...and why? ..." he asked.

"Yes," Noemi said cruelly. We not only thought that you knew, but that you vouched for him with your friend Kallina."

"My friend?" he shouted, opening his frightened eyes. He saw red. He shouted something else, but without knowing what he said, and ran out waving his cap as though going to put out a fire.

He found himself in the usurer's little courtyard.

Everything was as peaceful inside there as Noah's ark. White doves cooed with their coral claws in the architrave of the little door under a vine that cast a garland of gold on its black shadow; and in this frame the usurer was spinning, with her little stockingless feet in embroidered slippers, both sides of her kerchief folded over the top of her head.

Efix's agitation disturbed the peace of the place.

"Tell me right now about this business with Don Giacinto."

The usurer raised an eyebrow and looked at him placidly. "Did he send you?"

"The man that'll hang you sent me! Talk fast."

At his threatening gesture she stopped spinning. She was afraid, but didn't show it.

"Your *padrone* sent you then? Oh, well, tell them not to worry. There's time, I'm not in a hurry. Altogether I've given the boy four hundred scudi. He began asking me for money when we were at the festa. He wanted to make a good impression. He said he was expecting money from the mainland and left me a note signed by Don Predu. How could I say no? He came back later and told me he had played cards with Milese and lost. I told him I'd take the note to Don Predu. That scared him and he brought me another note signed by Donna Ester. Then I gave him more money. How could I say no? You didn't know anything about it?" she concluded, taking up her spinning again.

Efix was destroyed. He remembered that Donna Ester had secretly written to Giacinto to come; she was also capable of secretly signing the note. How would it be repaid? He felt unable to move, as though his legs were heavy and swollen with all the blood rushing there, leaving his heart and head and hands inert. How would it be repaid?

The usurer continued to spin and the doves to coo, and the chickens pecked at the flies on the rosy paunch of the piglets lying in the sun. The whole world was at peace. Only he was in agony.

"Ah, then you didn't know about it? I thought the ladies had kept part of the money to pay you. In fact, I wanted to suggest to Don Giacinto that he deduct the ten scudi you owe me, but in faith I then thought that it wouldn't do. But if you want to renew the note, we can put it all on one bill."

Efix made an effort to move. He tore off his hat again and began to hit her on the face with it, mad with desperation.

"Oh, damn you…oh, hangman hang you…oh, what have you done?"

The courtyard was in a turmoil. Doves flew to the roof, cats climbed the walls. Only the woman was silent so people wouldn't come running, but she bent over to escape the blows and defended herself with the spindle, jumping, moving backwards, and when she was inside the kitchen she grabbed an iron bar from behind the door with both hands and straightened up against the wall, as still and terrible as a Nemesis with her club.

And then it was she who made the man move backwards, threatening him under her breath: "Get out of here, murderer! Get out."

He stepped back.

"Go! What do you want from me? Do I go looking for you? All of you come here, to me, when hunger or vice moves you. Don Zame came, his daughters have come, his grandson has come. Even you have come, murderer! When you need something you are nice, but then you become as ferocious as a starved wolf. Get out."

Efix was at the gate, but she kept coming right behind him.

"In fact, I have to tell you I've run out of patience because of the way you treat me. Pay me in September when the notes come due, or I'll make a complaint. And if the signature's fake, I'll put the boy in prison. Get out!"

He went away, but not to go home. He just kept walking through the little deserted town under the sun. Stumbling over the volcanic rocks scattered here and there, he felt that the legendary earthquake had occurred that same morning.

He wandered around among the ruins, and he felt he should be digging to drag cadavers from the rubble, treasures from underground, but he couldn't he was so alone, so weak, so unsure where to begin.

As he passed the Basilica he saw it was open, and he went in. No mass was being said, but the guardian was cleaning the church, and the swish of the broom in the shadowy silence sounded like the ancient ladies of the castle passing by in their brocade dresses with rustling trains.

Efix kneeled at his usual place next to the pulpit, leaned his head against the column and prayed. The blood began to move in his veins again, but hot and heavy like lava. His fever affected everything: the oblique rays of silver dust falling from the ruined roof looked like white holes in the black floor, and the pale frescoed figures looked down, bent over, ready to break loose and fall.

The Magdalene leaned forward from her black frame into the limits of the unknown. Love, sadness, remorse and hope laughed and cried in her deep eyes and on her bitter mouth.

Efix gazed at her a long time and seemed to remember a life long ago, and she appeared to gesture for him to come near, to help her down, to follow her....

He closed his eyes. His head was trembling. He seemed to be walking with her on the sand along the river, under the moon. They walked and walked, silently, cautiously, until they reached the wide road by the bridge. There his vision became confused. Lia was sitting on a cart, hidden among sacks of cork. The cart disappeared into the night, but on the bridge, in the moonlight, Don Zame lay dead, lying in the dust with a swollen violet mark on the back of his neck like a bunch of grapes. Efix kneeled beside the cadaver and shook him. "Don Zame, get up! Your daughters are waiting for you."

Don Zame didn't move.

He sobbed so loudly that the guardian with the broom came over to him.

"Efix, what's the matter? Aren't you feeling well?"

He opened his frightened eyes wide and seemed to see Kallina again with the iron bar yelling "Murderer!" at him.

"I have the fever.... I feel like I'm dying. I want to confess...."

"You come here for that? As if you can't make your confession to Christ!" murmured the guardian smiling ironically; but once again Efix leaned his head against the pulpit column and with eyes raised toward the altar began to babble. Large tears rolled down his face toward his trembling chin until they fell on the ground drop by drop.

Giacinto was waiting for him at the farm, stretched out in front of the hut.

As soon as he saw Efix coming up with a basket in his hand that, although empty, seemed to be dragging him down, he realized Efix *knew everything*. So much the better! Now he would be free from the most shameful part of the weight crushing him: silence.

"Tell me," he said when Efix sat down in his usual place, still holding the basket. "Tell me!" he repeated more loudly, because the other one remained silent. "What now?"

Efix sighed. "Now?" My *padrone* are a little calmer because I promised to send you away, understand? They think the notes were really signed by Don Predu, and I didn't have the courage to tell them the truth because the signatures are false, aren't they? Oh, yes, is it true? Oh, Giacinto, what have you done? And now? You'll go to Nuoro? You'll work? You'll pay them off?"

"It's too much…it's a lot of money, Efix…. How can I?"

Leaning over him, Efix spoke in a low voice: "Go, child of God, go! I would have liked for you to stay, but if I tell you to go away, it's because there's no other choice. Remember the good things you said the other evening. You said: I want the best for my aunts, I want them to get back on their feet…. Those were my thoughts, too, when I heard you were coming. But instead! If you don't pay, the usurer will auction the farm or send you to jail for the false signatures, and *they* will have to go begging…. That's what you've done! I know you didn't mean to be bad. You who promised so many good things the other evening, you, child of God…."

Giacinto began to shiver. He raised his face to Efix bending over him, and they looked at each other desperately.

"I didn't do it to be bad. I wanted to earn something. But how can you in this town? You know how it is, you've stayed here in such...such...poverty....

"My aunts won't have to pay a cent," he continued, after a moment of anxious silence. "Yes, I had to sign Zia Ester's name because the usurer wouldn't give me credit. But I'll pay, you'll see. And if I don't I'll go to jail. I don't care.

"To jail? No, this I won't allow. No."

"Well, then, do you have any money, Efix?"

"If I had any I wouldn't be here like this! I'd have paid off the notes."

"Then what can we do, Efix? What can we do?

"Listen, you go back to the usurer and ask her to give you one hundred lire to get to Nuoro. Look for work there. The important thing now is to change directions, to get on your feet once and for all. Do you understand?"

But Giacinto, who up to the last moment had hoped the servant could help, didn't answer. He didn't say another word. He curled up in a ball like a sick animal, listened to the flying grasshoppers rustling in the dry leaves and stupidly watched them rub their iridescent wings together. Two of them fell on his hand, connected, green and hard as metal. He jumped. He thought of Grixenda. He thought that he would have to leave and never see her again, so poor as to give up even a creature so poor. He buried his face in the grass, sobbing without tears, his shoulders shaking convulsively.

VIII

It was Thursday evening and the usurer was not spinning for fear of *Giobiana,* the witch who appears only on Thursdays, who shows herself only to the nighttime spinners and who can be the source of evil.

She was praying, instead, as she sat on the doorstep under a garland of vines silver and black in the moonlight. Every time she looked around she thought she still could see, here and there on the wall of prickly pears, the green eyes of Efix shinning with anger. They were fireflies.

They were fireflies, but she too believed in fantastic things, in the supernatural life of night creatures. She remembered when she was a poor child and went begging and gathering twigs by the Castle ruins – and hunger and malarial fever stalked her like mad dogs – she remembered one time while she was walking on stones as sharp as knives in the crimson sun hanging above the violet mountains of Dorgali, a *signore* came up to her silently and touched her on the shoulder. His suit was the color of the sun and mountains, and he resembled one of Don Zame Pintor's sons who died young.

She had recognized him immediately: he was a Baron, one of the many ancient Barons whose spirits still lived in the Castle ruins, in the caves dug in the hill that went clear to the sea.

"Girl," he said with a foreign accent, "run to the midwife and ask her to come to the Castle tonight, because my wife, the Baroness, is having birth pains. Run, save a soul. Keep it secret. Take this."

Kallina was trembling, clinging to her bundle of sticks that looked like a black cloud against the crimson sky; therefore, she couldn't hold out her hand and the gold coins in the Baron's hand fell to the ground.

He disappeared. She threw down the bundle, picked up the coins as fearfully as a bird pecking bread crumbs, and ran away skipping and jumping; but the midwife, even when she saw the hot humid coins in her burning hand, spit on her face to chase away the fear and said laughingly: Go on, you've got the fever and you're delirious. You found those coins. They can still be found under the Castle. Give them to me and I'll make them grow."

Kallina gave them to her, except for one with a hole in it that she kept on a red ribbon around her neck.

"Go," she said to the woman. "Save a life. You're pretending not to believe it because I'm keeping the secret. But I'll keep it just the same."

And Kallina fell to the ground as though dead.

The midwife maintained as long as she lived that it had been a feverish illusion, but everyone knew she said that because Kallina wouldn't tell her secret.

In the meanwhile the money grew: it grew more every year like the green and red pomegranates she saw inside Don Predu Pintor's courtyard.

Then one evening she had felt – as old as she was – the same reaction of joy and terror she had felt that time when a young *signore* appeared before her, exactly like the baron. It was Giacinto.

And every time she saw him that dizzy feeling came back, the confused memory of a previous life, ancient and subterranean like that of the barons in the Castle.

Here he comes. Tall, dark, his face white in the moonlight. He enters, sits next to her in the doorway.

"Zia Kallina," he said with a stranger's voice, "why did you tell the servant my business?"

"He asked me. He attacked me and wanted to kill me."

"Kill you? For so little? Oh, that man and my aunts make such a fuss about their poverty, while some people *over there* go millions in debt and no one knows about it!"

The old woman wasn't at all interested in the people *over there*. "I had to grab the club to defend myself. Do you understand? The servant is ferocious. Don't trust him!"

Giacinto sat still a moment, looking at his hands covered with curly vine shadows. Then he started.

"I won't trust him. In fact, I want to leave. I can't live here any longer.... I'll earn some money. In forty days I'll give it all back, to the last cent. But right now you've got to give me money for the trip. I'll leave you another note."

"Who'll sign it?"

"*I* will!" he said resolutely. "*I* will! Trust me. Save a soul. Come on, hurry! And keep it secret."

He touched her shoulder just like the Baron, and she got up and went to get money from her cash box. Two fifty lire bills that she stroked for some time, looking at them in the moonlight and thinking that for Giacinto's trip one was enough. So she put one back. Through the little window above the box the high moon laid a silver ribbon on her rigid breast, and at her neck could be seen the golden coin threaded on a blackened ribbon.

Giacinto wasn't happy. What was that thin paper in comparison to the treasures of the great *signori* on the mainland? When the usurer said she didn't want him to sign the note, he understood that she was giving him charity, and he felt an intolerable anguish. It was as though he were again in the port captain's hall, waiting quietly.

"I'll give it back to you no later than tomorrow," he promised as he stood up.

And he went to Milese to tell him he was leaving the next day. Also there, through the doorway, he saw the white of the moon and the black shadow of the pergola. Milese's mother-in-law, sitting on the bench like a primitive queen, wasn't spinning because of the *Giobiana*, but was chatting with her feverish daughter and the pale women servants sitting on the ground next to the wall.

"My son-in-law went out a moment ago; he must have gone to Don Predu's," she said to Giacinto. "Are your aunts well? Give them my warmest greetings and thank them for the present they sent my brother the Rector.

"Black plums!" said a greedy servant. "Natolia, blast her, ate them all on the sly."

"I'll go up to the farm with you if you'll give me some more, Don Giacì, " said Natolia provocatively.

"Come whenever you like," he replied, but his voice was sad, serious, and her old mistress admonished her: "Stick to your own kind, Natolia!"

When he left them he felt the women were laughing and talking about him and Grixenda. Yes, he had to leave, to go seek his fortune.

In order not to pass in front of Grixenda's house, he went down one alley after another, until he reached an open space where the ruins of a Pisan-style church stood.

Euphorbia perfumed the air, the bluish moon shone on the ruined tower like a flame on a black candle, and it seemed like in that dead corner of the world day would never break again. Immediately beyond the open space was Don Predu's white house among pomegranates and palms like a Moorish residence, with arched doorways, loggias, and half-moon windows.

Giacinto crossed the large courtyard where wide reed lattices lay glittering in the moonlight. Beans, now covered with reed mats, were dried there in the daytime. Through a door Giacinto saw his uncle's large figure and Milese's thin shape in the golden background. Sitting in the quiet room, legs crossed and elbows on the table, they were drinking. Both the fat man and the thin one seemed happy with life.

"Have a drink, have a drink!" they said at the same time, offering Giacinto their glasses of wine, but he refused both.

"You're not drinking because you feel bad?"

"That's right, I feel bad."

However, he didn't say what was wrong; besides, those two wouldn't have understood.

"Did your Zia Noemi beat you?"

"Didn't Grixenda give you enough kisses? Blast you," Milese said, repeating the greedy servant's curse.

"Ugh!" Giacinto snorted, leaning his elbows on the little table and grasping his head in his hands. Don Predu observed how his shoulders trembled and his face slightly paled. That trembling of Giacinto's shoulders seemed to trouble him for he stood up and held out his hand:

"Let's go get some fresh air."

They went outside. Their steps echoed in the silence like the night patrol on its rounds. As they walked about Giacinto also got caught up in his companions' slightly ironic mirth.

"Shall we go to the theater, Zio Pietro? Night life begins at this hour in cities on the mainland. Carriages flow by the theaters like a black river. Ladies are even out walking their little dogs."

Milese laughed until he started hiccuping. Don Predu was more reserved, but his smile cut like a knife.

"Go back there, then! And drag Grixenda after you like a little dog."

"Ugh! How stupid you are in this town."

"Not as stupid as in yours, though."

Giacinto was silent a moment before he spoke. "Why do you call me stupid? Because I have a good heart? Because I want to enjoy my youth? And what do both of you do? Are you living? What kind of life do you have, Milese? You don't even love your sick wife. And you, Zio Pietro? What's your life? Storing money like beans on a mat for the pigs. You don't love anyone, not even yourself."

The two friends elbowed each other good naturedly. "You're really sick this evening: sick in your wallet."

"My wallet has more in it than yours does! Let's go to the tavern and you'll see," Giacinto said, blushing in the shadows.

"You wouldn't drink with us! I wouldn't touch your wine to save your life!"

Nevertheless they ended up in the nearly empty tavern. Two men were silently playing cards and a third was looking at the cards of one and then the other, but at a sign from Don Predu he came over to the newcomers and all four sat around another table.

The tavern keeper, a little townsman who looked like a Biblical Hebrew with his jerkin open over his oriental trousers, brought wine in a Levantine pitcher and put a black iron lantern in the middle of the table. Milese, head bent to the right, thoughtfully shuffled the cards, looking from one of his companions to the other.

"What's the stake?"

"Fifty lire," Giacinto answered.

He pulled out the usurer's money.

He lost.

The quiet, bluish flame in the black lantern looked like the moon over the ruined tower.

IX

One evening in July Noemi was sitting in her usual place in the courtyard, sewing. The day had been extremely hot and the gray-blue sky looked like it was covered with ashes from a fire whose last flames were dying out in the west. The flowering prickly pear provided a golden note in the gray of the gardens and over there behind the tower of the ruined church Don Predu's pomegranates looked like specks of blood.

Noemi felt all this gray and red inside herself. Her yearly spring-sickness hadn't ended with the coming of summer. In fact, with every passing day a stronger need for solitude forced her to hide in order to better devote herself to her torment, like someone sick who no longer hopes to get well.

That day she was alone. Ester and Ruth had accepted an invitation from the Rector to be part of a festival committee; Giacinto was in Oliena buying wine for Milese. Yes, he had come to that: to being a servant to someone who had once been a traveling salesman. Noemi despised Giacinto and never spoke to him, but when she was alone she saw him once again bent over her as he bathed her face with vinegar and tears, and heard his trembling voice say: "My dear Zia Noemi, why? Why this?" and his eyes, as sad and burning as that summer sky, never left her mind.

She could still taste his tears on her lips, and it was the taste of all human sadness, all human weakness. Then the image of him in his everyday demeanor – bored, confused, cowardly, impossible to control because of the impression he gave of a house-destroying boulder rolling down the mountain – would give way to the image of him as good, penitent, impassioned.

Yes, this was the image Noemi loved, and at times she felt it so vivid and real next to her that she blushed and cried as though grabbed by a lover who had secretly entered the courtyard.

Then her soul would thrill with passion. A whirlwind of desire would envelope her, carrying off all sad thoughts like the passing wind strips a tree of its dead leaves.

She felt she must have fainted, like on that day, and her tears were Giacinto's. She sipped them like the juice of bitter fruit with her greedy lips trembling from all the kisses that she had neither given nor received. Giacinto's youth, ardor, sorrow invaded her. Her years, appearance, essence were forgotten; she seemed to be lying under clear water in a thick woods and to be seeing a figure bent over to drink, to drink above her mouth. It was Giacinto, but it was also her, Noemi, alive, thirsting for love. It was a mysterious spirit drinking all the water from the spring, all the life from her mouth with an insatiable thirst. And then it stretched out in the hollow of the spring in the thick of the woods to form a single being with her.

A knock on the door called her back to the present. She went to open it, believing it was her sisters, or Giacinto himself, whose presence she did not fear because it was enough to break the enchantment. Instead she saw Zia Pottoi and instinctively closed the door to keep her out. The old woman pushed from outside.

"You want to squash me like a spider, Donna Noè! I haven't come to hurt you."

Noemi drew back, cold and indignant, looking at the piece of linen she held in her hand. "What do you want?"

"I want to talk to you, ma'am, but quietly, like one good person to another," the old woman said, straightening the corals on her dark neck, and she was trembling, fleshless as a skeleton.

"Donna Noemi, look at me! Don't look away. I've come to ask your help."

"Mine?"

"Yes, yours, ma'am. It's been three months since you and your sisters haven't allowed me to set foot in here. You're right. But last night I dreamed about Donna Maria Christina. I saw her beside my bed like she came that night I was given the last rites. She was beautiful, Donna Maria Cristina. She was wearing a kerchief as white as a lily. 'Go to Noemi,' she said, 'Noemi has my heart because the heart of the dead remain with the living. Go, Pottoi,' she said, 'You'll see that Noemi will help you.' Those were her very words."

At the door Noemi tried to continue sewing, with her head bent over the cloth that reflected the red of the sky over the mountain.

"Well, what do you want?"

"I'll tell you. You know all about it. The children love each other. I say: if they love each other why stop them? Didn't we love when we were young? But time passes, ma'am, and the boy is behaving strangely. My Grixenda's thin as a stick. He doesn't want her to go out of the house or work, and if he sees her on the doorstep he makes her go back inside. If Grixenda complains he says: 'I'm killing my aunts with sorrow because of you, especially Noemi.' He says that only because he is well behaved and good, but those words are like poison that eats away without causing pain."

She gave a big sigh and took the hem of Noemi's apron, rolling the edge between her dark fingers.

"Donna Noemi, ma'am, you have your mother's heart. I can tell you. When my father warned me that if I looked at Don Zame again he'd put my eyes out with his prod, I closed them, and Don Zame was as though dead for me. But Grixenda isn't like that. Grixenda can't close her eyes."

In spite of herself Noemi felt upset. The old woman rolling the hem of her apron like a child perturbed her.

"It's your fault," she said, gravely. "As old as you are, you know how these things end."

"We know, we know...and we never know anything, ma'am! The heart is never old."

"That's true," admitted Noemi, but with a voice that seemed to come from her mouth in spite of herself. However, she immediately scowled and fixed her cold mocking eyes on the old woman.

"Well, what do you want from me?"

"Speak with Don Giacinto. Yes, tell him: 'leave Grixenda in peace or marry her.'"

"I must tell him this? Why me?" Noemi asked, and as the other woman stared at her in turn without replying, she had an unpleasant impression: it seemed like the old woman knew. She lowered her eyes and began, harsh and cold: "I won't tell him anything! Just don't forget: you knew who he was, and you have been a bad grandmother to let Grixenda care for someone unsuitable for her."

"Why unsuitable for her? A free man is always suitable for a free woman if they are in love. And ma'am, yes, you will do me this favor and speak to him. I'm not asking you for bread. It's more than bread. It's a woman's salvation. The boy will listen to you because he's good and says: 'I don't want Zia Noemi to suffer because of me....' Well, then, I'll tell you the truth: he always talks about you and loves you. Grixenda is even jealous of you."

Then Noemi began to laugh, but she felt her knees tremble, and in her heart she felt the luminous beauty of the sunset. It was a sea of light spread over golden islands, with a mirage in the background. She had never felt such a moment of elation.

In an instant the world had changed appearance. The old woman looked at her, and in her vitreous eyes malice glittered like the youthful necklace on her skeletal neck.

"What are you saying, then, Donna Noemi? I can go home with a little hope? Yes, you'll really help me?"

"Certainly, go in peace," Noemi said in a changed voice; however, the old woman didn't leave right away, but bowed deeply in humble thanks.

"Our poor house has always been next to yours, like the servant next to her mistress. Our bad blood couldn't last!

My Zuannantoni cries every time I come back from the garden. He cries and says: why have the women chased me away? And he picks up his accordion and plays here behind the wall. He says he's serenading Donna Noemi. Have you heard him, ma'am? And now everything'll be all right."

"Let's hope everything will work out all right," Noemi said. But she didn't know what would be all right. She felt an impulsive love for everyone. "Tell Zuannantoni to come this evening. I'll give him some red pears."

The old woman took her hand, kissed it, and went back home in tears. The sky, pale in the east, still burned over Monte, as if the whole day's splendor was concentrated up there. Noemi persisted in her attempts to sew, but saw neither cloth nor needle. She only saw that great light, that boundless, deep, infinite, mirage. She seemed to hear the boy's serenade, and songs of love passed through the burning twilight air. Once again she could see the priest's rustic belvedere at the church of the Rimedio. A bonfire burned in the courtyard and the festivities grew more frenzied. All at once she too went to join the chain of dancing women. She too took part in the festival. She was the wildest of all. She was like Grixenda and Natolia and felt in her heart the ardor, sweetness, passion of all the women together. Giacinto squeezed her hand and the festival in the courtyard, in the world, was for them....

But little by little she woke up. The fire seemed to go out and the blood stopped beating violently in her veins. She remembered her promise to the old woman that "everything will be all right." Then she searched for the words to convince her nephew to get on the right track and marry Grixenda. She wanted them to be happy! She loved them both now: the woman because she herself was a part of the man with her love. May they be happy in their poverty and in their love, in their voyage toward a promised land. She loved them because she felt a part of them, joined to the man through her love, joined to the woman through her sorrow. She blessed them like an old mother, but she felt mysteriously transported with them, like Jesus with his parents in the flight to Egypt....

And like children and old people she began to cry without knowing why – in sorrow that was joy, in joy that was sorrow.

Someone knocked again, and she dried her eyes with the linen cloth and went to open the door. A man entered, closing the door behind him.

He was the bailiff, a thin man whose face was dark from a week's growth of beard. He had a long paper in his hand, folded in half. He raised his stiff green hat from his bald head and looked at Noemi, hesitating to speak.

"Donna Ester's not here?"

"No."

"I would.... I would have liked to give this to her. But I can give it to you," he said quickly, writing some lines with a pencil at the bottom of the paper and spelling out the words as he wrote.

"De-liv-ered – delivered, into, in-to the hands of the noble sister, Donna, Donna No-e-mi – Noemi Pintor."

She looked at him stiffly, inwardly trembling. A hundred questions rose to her lips, but she didn't want to appear curious and weak in front of that man who everyone in town feared and despised.

For his part, the bailiff hesitated again before giving her the paper until he finally did it and quickly went away.

Noemi began to read, with the linen cloth over her arm, her eyes still wet with tears of love.

"In the name of His Majesty the King...." The paper had something mysterious and terrible about it. It seemed to have come from a evil power.

Slowly, the more she read and understood, the more Noemi thought she was dreaming. She sat down and read it again. Caterina Carta, profession housewife, demands from noblewoman Ester Pintor, within five days from this notification, restitution of two thousand seven hundred lire, including cost of the note signed by the noble Ester Pintor.

At first Noemi thought, just as Efix, that Ester had acted rashly. A fleeting redness colored her forehead. Like a flame that glows a second and goes out in the distance of an obscure night, the certainty that she also would have, a few moments earlier, done something foolish for Giacinto rose from the depths of her conscience. Then silence, darkness. She, yes, a few moments before, but Ester? Ester wouldn't have been so foolish, Ester *wouldn't* have ruined the family out of love for that adventurer.

The truth flashed like lightning. It made her jump, run here and here, staggering, stumbling, as though struck by a physical pain.

The sisters found her in this condition.

Ester took the paper with the free hand outside her shawl. Because it was already dark, Ruth lit the lantern.

They all three sat on the bench and Noemi, recovering her calm and cruelty, read the paper aloud. The sisters' faces bent over the paper glistened with perspiration and anguish, but Noemi looked up and said: "Ester, if you didn't sign anything, we don't have to pay anything. That's clear. Why are you so miserable?"

"He'll go to prison."

"Too bad for him!"

"Noemi, what kind of talk is that? Can you send a man to prison?"

"Well, what do you want to do?"

"Pay."

"And then go begging?"

"Jesus asked for alms."

"Jesus also punishes sinners, frauds, and forgers."

"In the other world, Noemi!"

Ruth was silent while her sisters argued, but she was perspiring, leaning against the back of the bench, with her hands lying limply alongside her hips. For the first time in her life she had the strange feeling of needing to act, to do *something* to help the family.

"Oh," Ester said, rising and crossing the shawl over her breast, "after all we must be patient and prudent. I'll go to Kallina and beg her to wait."

"You, my dear sister? You to the usurer's house? You, Donna Ester Pintor?"

Noemi pulled her by the hem of her shawl, but although Ester had preached patience and prudence, she burst out: "Donna Ester my eye! Need, you know, my dear sister, makes everyone equal."

And out she went.

Noemi was struck once again with humiliation and indignation. The figure of Efix appeared before her like that of a resigned sacrificial victim, and she rushed into the courtyard and out the gate to wait for someone to pass that she could beg to go get the servant.

"He, he's the cause of everything! He promised to look after Giacinto and to protect us from him."

No one passed by. All was silent and inside the house Ruth seemed dead. Noemi never forgot that moment of waiting in the last twilight that seemed like the twilight of her life itself. Standing on the broken stones of the doorsill, she leaned forward and appeared to be waiting for a mysterious being, a savior and an avenger at the same time.

Footsteps resounded, slowly, heavily. A shape appeared down the street. As it came up the hill it grew larger, standing out gigantically against the colorless background of the horizon. It was black, except for a thread of fire that shone on his chest near his heart.

He reached Noemi, and noticing her agitation, stopped, while she leaned her open hand heavily against the wall in order not to fall, so much was she moved by the desire and horror to turn to the man.

He asked: "Noemi, what's the matter?"

She felt her heart bursting to call for help. "Predu, do something for me. Find someone who can go to the farm to get Efix."

"I'll go, Noemi."

"You? You? You…no."

"Why not?" he shouted. "Are you afraid I'll steal your watermelons?"

She continued to babble senselessly: "You, no...you, no...you, no...."

Don Predu guessed what was going on inside her.

He didn't know why for some time, from the evening he had brought the basket, from the evening when Giacinto had told him, "you store up money like beans for pigs," he had felt an emptiness, a strange illness, almost as though the stranger had communicated his sickness to him, and he felt an unusual pity for his cousins. He saw that Noemi was trembling and he, too, leaned a hand against the wall next to hers. Their faces were near each other; his had a masculine odor of sweat, of sunburned skin, of wine and tobacco; hers was a more subtle perfume of lavender and tears.

"Noemi," he said, gruff and shy, taking off his hat and then putting it back on. "If you need me, tell me. What happened?"

Noemi didn't reply. She couldn't speak.

"What happened?" he repeated more loudly.

"We're ruined, Predu...." she said finally, and she seemed to be speaking against her will. "We are lost. Giacinto forged Ester's signature.... And the usurer has called in the note...."

"Oh, damnation!" shouted Don Predu, pounding his fist against the wall.

Noemi was frightened by that shout and a feeling of propriety brought her back to herself. She thought the neighbors might be listening to her misery.

"Come inside, Predu: I'll tell you everything."

He went into the house where he hadn't crossed the threshold for twenty years.

The lantern was burning on the ancient bench, and the flame seemed to be sympathetic company to Ruth still sitting quietly with her head leaning against the back, her hands with their gnarled knuckles sprawled haphazardly. Half her face was illuminated, ashen; half was in shadow, black. Her half open eyes were looking upward, strained, as though in an effort to fix them on a distant point.

As soon as Don Predu saw her he started, but immediately got hold of himself. From his gesture Noemi knew the truth. She looked at him wide-eyed, then at her sister as she ran to her.

"Ruth, Ruth?" she called softly, bent over her, grabbing her by the shoulders.

Ruth's head fell first one way and then the other, then her whole body seemed to bend forward to listen to the voice of the ground calling her to itself.

The lament of Zuannantoni's accordion reached the bottom of the chaos of Noemi's pain like a distant light. The boy was singing, accompanying himself, and his hoarse voice of inexpressible melancholy filled the night with sweetness and light. Noemi, still kneeling near the bench where the Ruth's body lay, raised her face and looked around. She was alone. Don Predu had run to get Ester. She remembered the old woman's words, "Zuannantoni will come serenade you" and a howl of pain came from her colorless lips. Shouts, moans, laments mixed with the notes of the instrument and the boy's song, like the sobbing of something or someone left wounded in the woods, mixed with a nightingale's trill.

Suddenly everything was silent. Then footsteps and voices were heard. The courtyard was full of people. Noemi saw the boy beside her, with his pale face and big frightened eyes, hugging his accordion to his chest as though defending himself from attack, and she whispered in his ear: "Run. Go get Efix."

X

Ruth was gone. Shadows and silence surrounded the house once again.

Sitting on the stairs, holding a sprig of jasmine in his hand, Efix waited for Giacinto to return, feeling vaguely fearful.

Giacinto hadn't come back. Without a doubt he had learned of the disaster and was hesitant to return. Where was he? Still at Oliena, or at Nuoro, or further away?

Efix tried to gather his thoughts, memories, impressions of those three terrible days. Right now he still seemed to be sitting in front of his hut listening to the nightingale down there among the alder trees. That wave of harmony expanding to refresh the night sounded like the river's voice, and it was so melodious and heart-rending that the night spirits themselves remained quietly at the edge of the hill to listen. Efix felt carried away as by a gust of wind: memories and hopes lifted him up. He had been waiting for Giacinto, for Giacinto to come up with fantastic news: that he had found a job, that he had kept his promise to be his old aunts' consolation. And that Don Predu had asked Noemi to be his wife....

But instead of Giacinto it was Zuannantoni who had come with something black on his chest like a dead vulture. At that moment Efix felt like he was falling under the sway of feverish delirium. How terrible the wide white road at night, with the sound of the accordion descending from the hill that silenced even the nightingale! The sprites and monsters shook and danced in the shadow around him, following him, surrounding him.

And here he was waiting again. But even Giacinto had taken on a monstrous aspect, as if the nocturnal spirits had carried him away to their mysterious realm, and he would return horribly deformed.

Better never to return.

A little light from the kitchen illuminated part of the courtyard; some timid sounds could be heard inside. Donna Noemi and Donna Ester were moving around in there, but it sounded like they too were afraid, afraid of letting themselves feel alive.

When someone pushed open the front door all three, the women and the servant, jumped as though awakening from that dream of death.

It was the old Pottoi woman who came to ask news of Giacinto. She moved like a shadow, but must have left someone outside because she turned to look, while the women haughtily retreated.

"The boy has been away for five days and we don't know where he is! Tell me, Efix, dear, where he is."

"How can I tell you if I don't know myself?"

"Tell me, tell me," she insisted, bending over Efix and touching her necklace almost as though to take it off and give it to him. "Did you send him away? Did Donna Noemi send him away?... Tell me. You know. My Grixenda is dying...."

She bent over further, and above her shape as dark as a mountain Efix saw a star shining.

"What can I give you, dear Efix?"

"Nothing, old woman!" he said loudly. "I swear to you that I don't know anything! But as soon as he comes here I'll let you know."

"You're a good man, Efix! God will repay you. Come out here.... Comfort her."

She took his hand and drew him out. Grixenda was leaning against the wall and crying like someone who had lost everything good forever.

"Well, then, what's the matter with you? He'll come back."

"You hear that, my love?" said the old woman, pulling the girl away from the wall. "He'll come back. It's not like he went away forever, no!"

"Yes, he'll come back, girl."

Grixenda took his hand and kissed it as she sobbed. Her tear-wet lips left an impression on his fingers like a flower damp with dew. He started and the nightmare into which he had fallen for three days seemed to dissolve.

"He'll come back," he repeated in a loud voice. "And everything will be all right. He'll settle down and be sorry, you'll both be happy and everything will be fine."

The two women went away comforted. He went back inside and saw Noemi rise up before him like a black shadow.

"Efix, I heard you. Efix, don't get it into your head to kill us, too. Giacinto mustn't come back into this house."

Efix still held the jasmine in his hand and the little flower trembled in the dark, as from pain.

"Kill you.. me! Why?"

"Efix, I heard you!" she repeated in a monotonous voice. But suddenly her figure leapt, the shadow seemed to grow tall, enormous. Efix felt her on him like a tiger.

"Efix, do you understand? He must not come back here, not even to this town! You, you are the cause of everything. You let him come, you said you would protect us from him.... You...."

He took off his cap like a penitent.

"Donna Noemi, forgive me! I thought I was doing the right thing.... I was thinking: when I'm not here any more, they'll have someone who will protect them, at least."

"You? You? You are a servant and nothing more! You can't forgive us for being noble and you want to see us go begging with your *bisaccia*. But crows will eat your eyes first. You've seen two of us leave here...but you won't see the other two. You'll always be the servant and we the *padrone*...."

As though standing before a possessed woman he crossed himself and went to get his *bisaccia* to flee to the ends of the world; but Donna Ester stopped him with her hand, and Noemi, who had followed him, fell on the bench like Donna Ruth, with her eyes closed and her face violet.

He went outside and remained the entire night on the stairs with his face in his hands.

Before dawn he went in search of Giacinto. And up up, over the wide road first gray, then white, then rosy: the dawn seemed to rise from the valley like red smoke inundating the fantastic peaks on the horizon. Monte Corrasi, Monte Uddè, Bella Vista, Sa Bardia, Santu Juanne Monte Nou rose from the luminous hollow like petals of an immense flower opening in the morning; and the sky itself seemed to bend over it, pale and touched by such beauty.

After sunrise the enchantment vanished. Hawks shrieked overhead, their wings flashing like knives. Monte Orthobene showed its profile like a nuragic city facing the white bulwark of Monte Oliena, and between the two appeared Nuoro's cathedral on the horizon.

Efix walked with a feverish veil before his eyes. He felt like he was dead and walking, walking like a soul in torment that must still reach his eternal destiny; however, from time to time a sense of rebellion would make him stop, sit down on the guardrail and look off into the distance. The road rising between the valley and the mountain, among olive trees, prickly pears, rocks all the same gray color, seemed like his calvary, yes, but also a road that could lead to freedom. He was thinking as he looked at the shape of Monte Orthobene, over there is a granite city, with strong silent castles. Why not hide there, alone, and eat herbs and stolen meat, free like the bandits?

But from an open place in the valley he saw the Redeemer statue high on Monte Orthobene with the huge cross that seemed to join the blue sky to gray land, and he knelt down with bowed head, ashamed of his fantasizing.

Giacinto was at Oliena. He knew about the tragedy and death of Zia Ruth and was afraid to return. He lived with the few lire earned from the sale of the wine he bought for Milese, but he didn't know what to do next. He, too, was looking off into the distance from the little window of his room above the sloping courtyard, in the background of which, as from a hole, he saw the great Isporosile valley, with the cathedral of Nuoro in the background against a rose-streaked sky.

He couldn't even make up his mind to go to Nuoro. He felt like he was waiting for something that still had to happen, and on his meandering through town, drunk with sun, he would stop at the church door. The white village below the blue, clear mountains that seemed to be made of marble and air, burned like a lime cave, but every once in a while a stream of wind would cool him and the walnut and peach trees in the gardens murmured among the rustling of water and birds.

Giacinto would watch the women who had gone to mass – composed, stiff, with square faces pale in the frame of their hair shining like black satin, their bare deer ankles and beautiful flowered slippers. Sitting on the ground in front of the church, their red bodices almost completely covered by embroidered kerchiefs, they reminded him of a field of flowers. And the whole church was full of ribbons and idols: little black saints with pearl eyes, large and deformed saints more monstrous than idols.

After the holy functions the people would go home and Giacinto would return to his refuge, passing by a church ruin that reminded him of his aunts' house. He thought more about Zia Noemi than Grixenda and he wanted to cry, to go back there, to sit next to her as she sewed in the courtyard and put his head on her lap, under the linen cloth. But then he would feel ashamed of his fantasy and go back to the little window of his solitary room to look at the cathedral of Nuoro. Perhaps his salvation was over there.

Swallows' nests, stone-colored with time, ran like decoration between the roof and windows of the little house. In every nest were little birds. Every once in a while a shiny round head like a castanet would come out, one swallow and then another, ten, twenty, and everything was a fluttering of little black crosses, a melancholy screeching around Giacinto's window.

They would come so close to his face he would try to nab one, standing quietly in ambush. And so an hour would pass. But one day when he saw the tired figure of Efix coming up through the courtyard he realized that was what he was waiting for.

From down below the servant looked up without speaking. He was hardly able to open his mouth, but nodded in the direction of the road, indicating that Giacinto should follow him, and so Giacinto did.

They went behind the church and leaned against the crumbling wall, facing the great, light-filled countryside.

"Well, then?" Efix demanded in a trembling voice.

That made Giacinto laugh; he didn't know why, but in the face of the servant's misery he felt suddenly strong and wicked.

"You ask me 'well, then?' I ask you. What's new that makes you dog my steps? Did you come to buy wine for Zia Noemi's wedding?"

"Show respect to your aunts! You'll never see them again. Donna Ruth is dead."

Giacinto lowered his head then and looked at his hands.

"See? See? Not a word of sorrow! Not even a tear! And she died because of you, you dog."

Giacinto's shoulders began to tremble; his lower lip trembled, too, but he bit it angrily, and clenched and opened his fists almost as though wanting to take something and throw it away.

"What did I do?" he asked insolently.

Then Efix looked him up and down with sorrow and contempt.

"You have to ask? Why are you still here if you don't know what you did? I'm not telling you anything, I won't ask you why you don't feel anything. You don't even have a heart! I've just come to tell you never to put a foot in their house again!"

"You could have saved yourself the trouble! Who wants to go back there?"

"That's all you have to say? At least tell me what you intend to do. Your disgraced aunts are reduced to begging because of you. What do you intend to do?"

"I'll pay back everything."

"You? With promises! Oh, that's enough, for God's sake! You don't fool anyone anymore, you know! It's time to stop. Stop the pretense because anyway we don't have anything to give you. Do you understand, you good for nothing?"

Then it was Giacinto's turn to look him up and down, malicious and surprised. Then he raised his arms again and seemed to be coming up from the ground to strike Efix like an eagle attacking his prey. His teeth and eyes gleamed in the twilight, and his face grew fierce.

"Tell me, aren't you ashamed?" Giacinto asked in a low voice, grabbing his arms and looking hard into his eyes.

Efix felt his gaze burning into his pupils. He heard a roaring in his ears.

"Aren't you ashamed? You're the good for nothing! I may have made a mistake, but I'm young and can learn. Why do you come to torment me? I knew you'd come, and I was waiting for you. You should at least understand and not condemn me. Do you understand? You have nothing to say now? Oh, you're trembling now, you murderer? Oh, I'm ashamed I ever touched you."

Giacinto gave him a push and started on his way. Efix ran after him and grabbed him by the hand.

"Wait!"

They stood a moment in silence, as though listening to a distant voice.

"Giacinto! You have to tell me just one thing. Giacinto! I speak to you as a dying man. Tell me for your mother's sake! How did you know?"

"Why do you want to know?"

"Tell me, tell me, Giacì! For your mother's soul."

Giacinto never forgot Efix's eyes at that moment; eyes that seemed to implore from the depths of an abyss, while the hand that was squeezing his pulled him down toward the ground and the servant's body doubled over and slowly fell.

But Giacinto would not speak.

Efix let go of his hand. He fell grasping at the ground and began to cough and vomit blood, his face black and deformed. Giacinto thought he might be dying. He pulled him up and leaned him against the wall, looking down at him.

"Tell me! Tell me!" Efix groaned, lifting his bloody palms. "Was it your mother? Tell me at least that it wasn't her."

Giacinto shook his head no. Then Efix seemed calmer.

"It's true," he said in a low voice. "I killed him, yes, I killed your grandfather. A thousand times I would have confessed it in the street, in church, but I didn't do it because of *them*. If I weren't here who would help them? But it was an accident, Giacì! I swear it. I knew your mother wanted to run away, and I was sympathetic because I loved her. That was my first crime. I, a worm, a servant, dared to look at her. Then she took advantage of my affection, and used me to get away.... And *he*, her father, guessed everything. One evening he wanted to kill me. I fought back. I hit his head with a rock. He spun around like a top, with his hand on the back of his neck, and landed far from the place where he attacked me.... I thought he did it on purpose.... I waited.... I waited for him to get up.... Then I began to sweat...but I couldn't move.... I thought he was pretending.... I watched him for a long time. Finally I went up to him.... Giacì? Giacì?" Efix repeated two times, his voice low and breathless, as though still calling his victim. "I called him.... He didn't answer. I couldn't touch him.... And I ran away; then I went back.... Three times like that.... I never could touch him. I was afraid...."

Giacinto listened, tall, dark against the red sky. He was shaking and Efix, from below, thought the whole horizon was trembling.

But suddenly Giacinto went away without saying a word, and Efix saw open space before him, the rosy valley furrowed with shadow right up to the hills of Nuoro black against the sunset.

An infinite silence reigned. Only swallows' cries seemed to come out of the crumbling walls, and a horse could be heard trotting away into the distance.

"It's Giacinto," Efix thought. "He's taken a horse and he's going back there to mistreat his aunts and tell them everything."

He listened. It seemed to him that the sound of horse hoofs bounced off the wall above him; and then lower, on his body above his heart.

"He went off without saying a thing! But I didn't act that way when he told me his story about the captain!"

Suddenly he jumped up as if something had stung him. He brushed the dust off his clothes and ran behind the church, down to the big road, dogged by the thought that Giacinto might go back to the house to mistreat the women.

But when he arrived the house had fallen back into its death-like peace.

Donna Ester was washing the wheat before sending it to the mill, dipping a sieveful into a cauldron of water. The pebbles remained in a corner and she shook the sieve to get rid of them. The wheat was very dusty and full of little pebbles. It was their last sack.

But what struck Efix was seeing Donna Noemi with Donna Ruth's white kerchief on her head, a sign of mourning.

She had aged, as white as the mended sheet she was mending again.

He sat on the bench facing them. All three seemed as calm as if nothing had happened.

"Did he leave, or not?" Noemi asked.

"He will leave."

She stared at him. He was so gray and scrawny that she took pity on him and said no more.

For eight days all three had lived in the desperate hope that Giacinto might come back to make up for what he had done wrong, that Giacinto might leave and never show his face again!

XI

One autumn day Efix went to Don Predu's house.

Only the servants were there. One fat, elderly woman who gave herself important airs, like the Rector's sister and another woman, young and active, even though afflicted with malaria. Efix had to wait in a room on the first floor, and amused himself by looking at the reed trellis covered with green and black figs, violet grapes, and a split tomato veiled with salt in the large courtyard. The whole house breathed peace and well being. Against the white walls palm shadows trembled, and among the gilded leaves of the pomegranates the split red fruit showed their pearly seeds like baby's teeth. Efix thought of the desolate house of his poor mistresses, of Noemi who was consumed inside like a flower at dusk....

"You're so thin," the elderly servant said to him, sitting next to the door spinning. "Do you have the fever?"

"It can eat my flesh and bones, for the love of God," he sighed looking at his dark trembling hands.

"Are your *padrone* well? I don't see them anymore, not even in church."

"They don't go to church, since the tragedy."

"And Don Giacinto isn't coming back?"

"He's not coming back. He has a job in Nuoro."

"Yes, Don Predu saw him recently. But it doesn't sound like a very important job."

"It's enough to live on, Stefana!" Efix admonished, without raising his head. "It's enough live on without sinning."

"That's difficult, dear soul! How can you wade across the river without getting wet?"

"By crossing the bridge," said the other servant from the courtyard, bent over to shell a pile of almonds. Then she asked: "And Grixenda?"

Efix didn't reply.

"And does Don Predu still go to their house?"

"I don't know. I'm always at the farm."

The women were burning with curiosity, because for some time their *padrone* had sent gifts to his cousins and although he made fun of them, he didn't let anyone else speak badly of them in his presence. But Efix was not in the mood for confidences. Don Predu had sent someone for him, and he was there to wait for him, not to chat. The fever and weakness made a buzzing in his ears; it sounded like the murmur of the river in the night and distant voices. He had a world all his own inside his head where he lived detached from the real world.

Efix cared nothing about Giacinto any more, or even Grixenda, and almost nothing about his *padrone*. Everything seemed far away, always farther away, as if he were on a boat, and from the gray and turbulent sea he were watching the land fade away on the horizon.

But Don Predu was coming. He was thinner, as though somehow drained. The gold chain hung over his heaving stomach.

Efix got up and wouldn't sit down again.

"I have to go," he said, motioning toward the door like someone who had a long walk ahead of him.

"You have a lot of business to take care of? Or are you going to some festival?"

Don Predu's sarcasm didn't wound him any more; nevertheless the mention of a festival shook him.

"Yes, I want to go to the feast of San Cosimo and San Damiano."

"Well, then, you'll go! I suppose you won't be going immediately. Sit down. I want to ask you something. Stefana, wine!"

Efix, however, refused the glass with a gesture of horror. No drinking ever again, no vices ever again. He had fasted for two months and sometimes when he was thirsty he wouldn't drink for penitence. He sat down resignedly, looking at his hands; and Don Predu, after looking toward the courtyard to make sure the servants weren't eavesdropping, asked him quietly:

"Tell me how my cousins are getting along."

Efix looked up and immediately looked away. A dark blush colored his face so dry and fleshless that only skin seemed to cover his skull.

"My *padrone* have no more confidence in me and they don't tell me anything about their business. That's only right. I'm the servant. What's there to tell me?"

"Blast me, that they'll pay you. But they don't pay you! They need to tell you that at least. How much do they owe you?"

"Let's not talk about it, Don Predu! Don't shame me."

"You shame yourself, old man! Oh, well, listen. Sometimes I go visit those women, but it's impossible to get anything out of them. Ester might talk, but there's Noemi hard as a rock. The first evening after Ruth's unfortunate passing I went there by chance and that's the only time she ever confided in me. I know, by God, it was a desperate time. But afterwards the hostility returned. When I go there she's friendly enough, but every once in a while she gives me fierce looks, like I was the cause of their undoing. And if Ester opens her mouth to say something, Noemi gives her such a terrible look that it takes the words right out of her mouth."

"Just like with me," Efix said. "Just like that."

He almost felt a sense of relief, because the memory of Noemi's eyes persecuted him more than his old remorse.

"Now, listen to me. Seeing that I couldn't get anything out of them, I went to Kallina. But even she, damn her, wouldn't talk. She knows how to take care of herself, that damned soul. She pretends to believe that Ester really signed Giacinto's note and will only say that she wants what's hers. I know you and Ester have tried to straighten things out with her and that Kallina renewed the note for three months, with the addition of the expense for the protest and a higher interest, and has taken a mortgage on the farm. She's got a stranglehold. Yes, all right; but what'll you do now, in October?"

"I don't know. They haven't told me anything."

"I know Ester is making the rounds in search for money. She has a way to go: her teeth will fall out before she finds it. I know she'd even be willing to sell, but not to me."

Efix looked at his fingers and kept silent. Irritated by this indifference, Don Predu slapped his knees.

"What do you think, wooden statue? Oh, what do you say?"

"Well, then, I'll tell you the truth. I hope Giacinto will be able to pay."

Then Don Predu reversed himself, laughing from where he sat, his chest puffed out, his teeth glistening from fleshy lips. Even his fingers entwined with the gold chain on his chest seemed to laugh.

Efix looked at him with fear, his eyes filled with the anguish of a wounded animal.

"But what if that one dies of hunger! I saw him the other day. He looked like a tramp, with holes in his shoes. He even sold his bicycle. I won't tell you the rest!"

"No, tell me! Did he steal?"

"Steal? Are you crazy? Now even you slander that little flower, that painted angel. What would he steal? He's not even good at that."

"Well...what did he say? Is he coming back?"

"If he gets an idea like that in his head I'll break his neck," said Don Predu, his face darkening. Suddenly Efix had the feeling that his unfortunate *padrone* had finally found help, a stronger defender than he. Oh, God be praised. He doesn't abandon his creatures. Then his old hopes suddenly resurfaced: that Don Predu would marry Noemi, that the women's house would rise from its ruins. But his joy was extinguished as suddenly as it had caught fire, and again he found himself in his desert, on his sea, on his mysterious and terrible voyage toward divine punishment. All the grandeurs of the earth, even if they touched him, even if he became king, even if he had the power to make everyone in the world happy, wouldn't be enough to cancel his sin, to free him from hell. So how could he be happy? He returned to looking at his hands to hide the idea firmly fixed in his eyes.

Don Predu went on: "Giacinto won't come back, much less pay, I'll guarantee that. But remember what I've told you a thousand times. I want the farm. I'll pay everything, so the house will remain theirs. Try to convince them, those wooden heads. I'll keep you in my service...."

"Why don't you speak to them yourself? They don't listen to me."

"And they listen to me? I've tried to talk about it, but it's like talking to a wall. You have to convince them," the man said emphatically, slapping his knee again. "If it's true that you want the best for them, that's the only way. You *must,* it's your duty to open their eyes if they're blind. You *must*, do you understand or not? Do you have bugs in your ears?"

In fact, Efix looked as if he were in the closed world of the deaf. *Must*?

Was Don Predu threatening him? Did Don Predu know something? Nothing was important to him, he wasn't afraid of hell; nevertheless, he thought Don Predu was right.

"What must I do?"

"You have to show you're a man for once. You have to tell them that if they don't want to pay you with money, they can at least pay you with gratitude. If the farm gets into the hands of another owner you'll be thrown out like a dog. Then, yes, God help me, you'll go to the festivals, but with the beggars!"

Efix started. That was his dream for penitence. He got up and said: "I'll do everything. But the only thing...."

"The only thing?" asked the man, grabbing onto his sleeve. "Sit down, devil, and drink. The only thing?"

"Would be for Your Lordship to marry Noemi."

And Don Predu again swelled up with laughter. He was laughing, but he held on to Efix to keep him from leaving.

"How funny you are, you devil! I'll keep you with me all your life, so you can cheer me up when I'm in a bad mood! I'll let you marry Stefana. She's a little fat for you, maybe, but she's not dangerous, because thirty years have passed by for some time.... Stefana, Stefana," he shouted, keeping a firm grip on him and turning his smiling face toward the door. "Listen, here's a suitor for you."

The woman came to the door, dark, with a swollen belly and breast and a face as severe as a grandam. Efix glanced at her beseechingly.

"Don Predu wants to have a laugh."

"A bad sign when he wants to have a laugh. Others have to cry," the woman said, challenging her *padrone*'s look. And smiling behind her, pale and enigmatic, with her wide mouth closed tightly as though held firm by two dimples, was Pacciana, the other servant.

"I'm telling you that you'll marry Efix, Stefana. You say no now, but later you'll say yes. What's there to laugh about?"

"The sardonic laugh!" Pacciana cursed in a low voice behind her, and goaded Stefana to talk back to the *padrone*. But the woman was too dignified to go on with the joke. She didn't open her mouth until Don Predu and Efix went out together.

Then the two servants began to talk about Predu's cousins.

"When I go there with a gift in a basket, they receive me like I was coming to beg. But I'm the one bringing it to them! Did you see how hungry Efix looked? They haven't paid him for twenty years, and now they don't even give him anything to eat. Did you hear how Predu flew off the handle when he mentioned his two cousins?"

"Times change. Even colts grow older," Stefana pronounced sententiously. But both felt something new, serious, take over their destiny as servants without a mistress.

In the meanwhile, Don Predu accompanied Efix high up the road washed by the last rain.

Grass grew along the walls surrounding deserted houses. A sweet, profound silence enveloped everything. Yellow clouds looked down on damp Monte, and above the town, spreading out before the Pintor women's front door the plain with its gilded reeds and green river meandering among islands of white sand could be seen. The silence was such that the women beating their clothes down below there, under the solitary pine on the shore could be heard. Old Pottoi, standing silently in her doorway was looking, with one hand against the wall and the other shading her eyes. She seemed small, decrepit, with her jewels more gaudy and dismal than ever on her skeleton body.

"What are you doing?" was Don Predu's greeting.

"I'm waiting for Grixenda who went to the river. I didn't want her to, to tell the truth, because the boy, your nephew, forbid her to, and if he finds out he'll be hurt. But Grixenda does as she pleases."

"What? Has Giacinto written you?"

"Written who? He's never written. We don't know anything about him, but he'll come back, because he promised to."

"Sure. The dead come back, too, according to you!"

But the old woman turned to Efix standing there looking down at the ground.

"Didn't he tell you he'd marry her? Speak up. Did he tell you or not?"

Efix looked at her quickly, as he had looked at Stefana, and didn't answer.

"What I don't like is the unfriendliness of those women," the old woman said, looking down there again. "They send us away, and only Zuannantoni can sometimes enter their house closed tighter than the Castle in the Barons' time. They've forgiven Kallina, plague take her, but not us. Our Lady of the Rimedio help them. But when the boy comes back everything will be all right. Even Donna Noemi said so."

The two men went on their way, but the old woman called Don Predu back and said to him quietly: "Could you do me a favor? Tell Grixenda not to go to the river? It isn't dignified for someone who'll marry a *signore*."

Don Predu opened his thick lips to laugh and make one of his usual insolent remarks, but he looked down at the trembling old woman, looked at her necklace and dangling earrings, and he touched the gold chain, his face darkening like on that evening when he saw his nephew's shoulders tremble.

He rejoined Efix and they stopped in front of the women's closed front door. Nettles were growing on the steps. Don Predu was remembering the time Noemi was there waiting in the shadows.

"Well, do we understand each other? You must do as I say, understand?"

"I understand. I'll do everything," Efix said.

He knocked, but no one opened the door. Don Predu stood there touching his chain and looking down at the river almost as though he were expecting someone.

"Oh, are they dead, too?"

"Donna Ester might be in church and maybe Donna Noemi is lying down."

"Why, isn't she feeling well?"

"Mah! For quite a while she's been in bed every time I've come. She has headaches."

"Well, then, she should go out and get some fresh air."

"I think so, too, but where?"

Don Predu looked down toward the river. His face seemed different, almost handsome, sad and distracted, like his nephew's.

"Oh, she could go some place. To Badde Saliche, even to my farm toward the sea. There are still some white grapes...."

Efix's face brightened; he wanted to say something, but he heard someone opening the door, and Don Predu stepped back without turning, trying to hide next to the wall.

XII

Much to Efix's surprise, Donna Ester agreed to her cousin's proposal. And so the little farm was sold and the note paid. But something happened that set everyone in the little town talking. Efix, while continuing in the service of Donna Ester and Donna Noemi, became a share cropper on the farm. And so he brought his portion of produce to his *padrone*. Finally, gossipy women were saying that he had gone from the position of servant to the level of relative, or rather to that of the Pintor women's protector.

What was even more surprising was Don Predu's agreeableness, but he had seemed like another person for quite a while. He had even lost weight and a strange rumor circulated that he was "touched by a book," meaning bewitched by a charm performed with books of the saints.

Who would benefit from that?

No one knew. These things are never clear cut, and if they were they would no longer be great and mysterious. The fact was that Don Predu was losing weight, was much less insolent with his neighbors and was even so foolish as to buy a worthless farm, and with the farm he got the servant who could do as he pleased.

Stefana and Pacciana said: "He wants to give his unfortunate cousins charity."

But privately they agreed that since Don Predu continued to send presents to the Pintor women he did seem bewitched, and they talked about Efix in whispers: everything in the world is possible, and Efix loved his *padrone* to the point of making him capable of doing some magic charm for them. Above all, his comings and goings with Don Predu raised the servants' suspicions. Stefana looked to see if there was some magic object hidden under the threshold, and one day

Pacciana found a black pin in their master's bed.... Extraordinary things were bound to happen.

During winter the Pintor sisters kept to their house and never spoke of going to the Feast of the Rimedio, but as the days lengthened and the grass grew tall in the old cemetery, Donna Ester also seemed overcome by a sense of tiredness, by a languorous sickness such as made Noemi pale every spring. She almost never went to church, she dragged herself here and there through the house, sitting down every once in a while with her hands limp at her sides, complaining that her feet hurt. Their poverty was not as bad as in past years since Efix provided the necessities, but the air itself seemed impregnated with sadness.

During Lent the two sisters went to confession. It was a beautiful, clear, golden morning. Children's shouts and the flocks' bells could be heard in the reeds on the plain below, and the ever louder voice of the river sounded menacing but only in jest. Not a cloud in the completely blue sky, and the air so transparent that the Castle stones sparkled and an empty blue window in the ruins looked out from an ivy garland.

Father Paskale was inside his confessional and didn't intend to leave it, even though Natolia was waiting in the sacristy with coffee and cookies in a basket.

Seeing two new penitents arrive, the servant made a gesture of despair, and thought it best to go reheat the coffee at her friend Grixenda's house. And so she goes with the little basket on her head, passing behind the apse and down the lane between blackberry bushes sparkling with dew.

Through old Pottoi's open door one could see Grixenda bent over the flame of the *focolare* to boil coffee for her grandmother who was sick in bed.

"You get skinnier every day," Natolia said as she entered.

In fact, Grixenda was thin and pale – still young, but as though dried up. Certain movements of her skinny neck and yellow face resembled her grandmother's. Only her eyes shone large and clear, full of melancholy light and treachery, like the swamp water down there in the reeds on the plain.

"The coffee is getting cold. Now that those women have come it will be ice cold," Natolia said, taking the coffee pot from the basket. "I'll have a little bit, too."

"Those women! They should be horse whipped! And you along with them! If they dump out their whole sack of sins, you'll find Father unconscious inside the confessional."

"What a tongue! It's obvious a viper bit you. Here, take a cookie. I offer it to you like a flower to sweeten your heart."

But Grixenda really had a poisoned heart and couldn't take teasing.

"If you've come to prick me, Natolia, you've made a mistake. You don't have thorns, because you're an euphorbia, not a rose. I don't have aches and pains, I don't have worries. I'm strong as the pine tree on the river bank. The day will come when you'll beg to be my servant."

"Who would you marry? The Baron of the Castle?"

"I'll marry a live man, not a dead one. You can have the dead ones!"

"I think it was you who bewitched Don Predu."

"If I wanted to I could even marry Don Predu," Grixenda said, looking up fiercely with her tragic, childish face. "But I have other things in mind!"

As Natolia looked at her she felt sorry for her. Grixenda seemed beside herself, unhappy, and therefore Natolia quit tormenting her. She got another cookie and took it to Zia Pottoi in her dark hole. A streak of light rained from the roof of the little room, illuminating the bed where the old woman lay fully dressed and wearing the necklace and earrings, stiff and as still as a cadaver dressed for burial.

Thinking her asleep, Natolia touched her burning hand. But the old woman drew it back, saying under her breath: "Listen, Natolia, do me a favor. Go to Efix Maronzu and tell him I have to speak to him. But don't let Grixenda know. Go, little dove, go!"

"And where will I find Efix? Is he in town?"

"He's coming up from the farm. I see him coming up," said the old woman, putting a finger to her lips because Grixenda was coming in with the coffee.

"Look, Natolia, she wanted to get up this morning, and she has a high fever. Grandma, grandma, get back under the covers."

"I will, I will. We'll all get back under the covers," the old woman said, and Natolia went away with a heavy heart.

Strangely enough, while she was passing the Pintor women's house she saw Efix coming up the solitary road. He was bent under his *bisaccia,* so bent he seemed to be looking for something on the ground.

"The old woman must die and already *sees*," Natolia thought.

He looked at her with his eyes as indifferent as an animal's, and didn't say whether he would go to the old woman or not. Learning that the women were at confession, he took off his *bisaccia*, put it on the step and sat down to wait for them. The nettles pricked his hands.

Natolia then went back to the church and looked in to see if she could tell the women that their servant had arrived, so they would let the priest go. But Donna Ester was at one side of the confessional with the edge of her shawl sticking out like a black wing, and Donna Noemi was at the other side, her back undulating occasionally under the black opaque material, with a long, nervous foot sticking outside her skirt.

Other penitents were here and there praying, crouched on the green floor. A profound silence, a bluish light, the odor of grass invaded the Basilica as damp and desolate as a cave. Looking out from her frame, the Magdalene seemed to concentrate on the spring voices coming in with the fragrant air, and even Noemi inside there, next to the grate that emitted an odor of rust and human breath, felt a tremor of life, a desire for death, an agony of passion, an anguish of humiliation, all the yearning, regrets, rancor, and anxiety of a sinner in love.

On their return they saw Efix get up with difficulty, supported by a hand on the step. Then Noemi, still warm with piety and love of God, noticed for the first time that their servant was in a bad way, old and gray, with clothes grown too baggy, and she held out a hand to help him. But he was already up and paid no attention to her offer.

When they went into the house Ester asked for news of the farm as though it still belonged to her. He replied by raising his shoulders with uncustomary rudeness and went to wash at the well.

April had even cheered up the sad courtyard. Swallows poked their dark little heads from the nests on the balcony, watching their companions flying low as though following their shadow on the thick grass of the ancient cemetery.

"Efix, you don't look too well. You should take something, or give yourself a day of rest," Noemi said.

"Oh, yes, Donna Noemi? And what if I took a walk instead!"

"I said you don't look well. Don't joke. What's wrong?"

He looked at her with bright clear eyes, and his sudden joy made the wrinkles crinkle around his eyes.

"I'm getting old," he said, clapping his hands; and his joy went away as suddenly as it had come.

He had come back to town because Don Predu had sent for him. Otherwise he wouldn't have moved from the farm. What could Donna Noemi's pity do to help his problem? Nothing but make it worse.

Then he went to his new *padrone* and found him on a step ladder pruning the vine under a network of pomegranate branches decorated with little golden leaves.

There, too, swallows crisscrossed quickly, but higher up, against the sky's milky background. In the house the women could be heard cleaning rooms and putting everything in order for Easter, and a great peace reigned everywhere.

Efix never forgot that moment. He had left the farm with the certainty that something extraordinary was about to happen, but looking up at the feet on the ladder it seemed to him that Don Predu was sad too, almost sick, and that he hesitated before descending with the shining sickle in one hand. In his other hand a spray of vine dripped purple from its cut ends like blood from a cut finger.

"Wait until I finish, or are you in a hurry to go?" said Don Predu, but he suddenly seemed to remember something, and came down heavily, letting Efix put the ladder away.

"Well, now," he began when they were inside the house full of sun and shadows of swallows. "I have something to tell you...." and he hesitated, looking at his fingernails. "I want to marry Noemi."

Efix began to tremble so hard that his hand on the table seemed to jump. Then Don Predu began laughing his awkward, evil laugh of days gone by.

"I didn't think you wanted to marry her! I'm saving Stefana for you, you know!"

Efix remained silent. He looked at him with eyes so full of passion, terror, joy, that Don Predu turned serious. But he tried to joke again.

"Why are you getting so riled up? You're hoping I'll pay you what they owe you? No, you straighten that out with Ester. And then there's something else...."

He scrapped a spot off on his vest with his fingernail, looking up attentively.

"Now, then, will she want me?"

"Oh! Of course!" stammered Efix.

"Don't be so certain! Let's be serious. I thought about it a lot before I made up my mind. Believe me, I'm doing it more out of duty than caprice. What can I expect? Where can I turn? At my age a much younger woman isn't suitable. But that's not important. Anyway, I've made up my mind. Well, I won't deny it: Noemi is nice and I like her. To tell the truth, I've always liked her. But, what can I say? Life goes by and we let it pass like water in the river, and we only notice it when it's gone. But never mind," he added, slapping his knees, and then he got up and sat down again. "The important thing now is to find out if Noemi will accept me. I'll ask her the right way. I'll send Father Paskale, or the doctor or whoever; but I don't want to be refused. Oh, God help me, not that. You understand, Efix?"

Efix understood very well, and nodded yes, yes, his eyes shining. "Should I speak to Donna Noemi?"

Don Predu slapped his knees. "Bravo! That's what I want. And the sooner the better, Efix! We can't let these things turn sour. Say to her: 'Who should come to ask the official question? Father Paskale, his sister, or who?' If she says not to send anyone, so much the better, by faith, so much the better! And then we'll get things done in a hurry, without fuss. We aren't children any more. What do you think about that? I'll be forty-eight in September and she should be around thirty-five, what do you say? Do you know her exact age? Oh, then tell her she doesn't have to worry about a thing. The house is ready, there are servants – gossips, yes, but they're servants, and well paid. There's linen, there's everything. There are plenty of provisions, may God preserve them! That's all. Then we'll talk about these things with Ester. The only thing I don't like.... Oh, well, I can tell you, is that Ruth died like that.... Maybe she would have been happy, too...."

Efix got up. He felt something stinging him all over, and he needed to go, to hasten destiny along.

"Wait a little longer, you old devil! I'll give you something to drink. A little acquavite? Or anise? Stefana, God's curse. Here's your suitor, Stefana!"

The women could be heard banging furniture in a frenzy. Finally the old servant appeared with a napkin on her head and another in her hand, serious and imposing nevertheless, with her eyes full of resignation to her *padrone*'s will. She opened the cabinet, poured the anise and looked at Efix with a vague sense of terror, but also in order to discover if he took his employer's teasing seriously. But Efix was so humble and flustered that she went back and said to her young companion: "If he has cast some spell he did it well. Fortune falls like an arrow on those people. Do a good cleaning job so we won't have much to do for the wedding."

"Yours with Efix?" Pacciana asked. "Don Predu has to wait for Donna Noemi to accept him first!

But Stefana gave her the finger, so absurd did those words seem to her.

After Don Predu accompanied him to the door like a friend, and he was on the road again, Efix looked around and sighed.

Everything was different: the world had expanded like the valley after a big wind when the fog lifts and disappears. The Castle against the blue sky, the ruins where the grass trembled full of pearls, the plain down below with rust-brown reeds, everything had a sweetness of childhood memories, of things long lost, long lamented and desired and then forgotten and then finally found again when remembered and no longer regretted.

Everything is sweet, good, dear. The blackberries of the Basilica covered by spider webs, green and violet with dew; the gray walls, the corroded gate, the ancient cemetery with the white bone flowers amid wheat and thistles; the lane and hedge with lilac butterflies and red ladybugs that look like little flowers and berries. Everything is fresh, innocent and beautiful like when we are children and escape the house to run through the marvelous world.

The Basilica was open during these Lenten days, and Efix went to kneel in his place below the pulpit.

The Magdalene, also happy, was watching like the Barons' Spanish guest looking from the Castle balcony. She also felt spring, she was happy even though these were the days of Our Lord's passion. Some rich feudal lord must have asked her to be his bride, and she smiled at the passers-by from his balcony, and was also smiling at Efix kneeling below the pulpit.

"Lord, I thank you, Lord. Take my soul now; I'm happy to have suffered, to have sinned, because I experienced your divine Pity, your pardon, your help, your infinite greatness.

Take my soul, like a bird takes a grain of wheat. Lord, scatter me to the four winds. I will praise you because you have filled my heart...."

And yet, on wearily rising with his stiff knee he felt a sense of pain, as if the shadow of a cloud were passing in the church, veiling the Magdalene's face.

Donna Noemi's face, bent over her sewing in the courtyard, was also veiled with shadow.

Efix picked a pansy from the edge of the well and gave it to her. She looked up in surprise and did not take the flower.

"Guess who sent it? Take it."

"You picked it. You keep it."

"No, really, take it, Donna Noemi."

He sat down on the ground before her with his legs crossed like a slave, taking his feet in his hands. He didn't know how to begin, but he knew that she had already guessed. In fact, Noemi had let the pansy fall in the white valley of the cloth. Her heart was pounding. Yes, she had guessed.

"Where is Donna Ester?" asked Efix, bending over his feet. "How happy she'll be when she finds out! Don Predu had me come back to town for this."

"What are you saying, you wretched man?"

"No, don't call me wretched. I'm as happy as if I were dying in God's grace at this moment and saw heaven open. I went to church before coming here, to thank the Lord. I swear that's the way it is."

"But why, Efix? she asked in a weak voice, sticking her needle into the pansy. "I don't understand."

He looked up and saw her pale face with trembling lips and dark eyelids like a dead woman's. It's certainly joy that makes her so pale, and he felt a shiver, a desire to kneel before her and tell her: yes, yes, it's a great joy, Donna Noemi, let's cry together.

"You accept, Donna Noemi? You're happy, aren't you? Can I tell him he can come?

She made a violent movement. She bit her lip, opened her eyes and the blood returned to her face, but only slightly, merely around her eyes and lips. She looked at Efix, and he saw her eyes again, as in those terrible days, full of rancor and pride. The shadow fell over him again.

"Don't be offended if I talked to him first, Donna Noemi! I'm a poor servant, yes, but I'm as closed as a letter. If you accept, Don Predu will send a priest to make the offer, or whoever you want...."

Noemi threw down the wilted pansy and began to sew again. She seemed calm.

"If Predu wants a laugh, let him laugh. I don't care."

"Donna Noemi!"

"Yes, yes! I'm not saying he isn't serious. Otherwise you wouldn't have gone there. But now please get up and go away."

"Donna Noemi?"

"Well, what's wrong with you now? Get up, don't stay there on your knees with your hands like you're praying! You're stupid!"

"But Donna Noemi, what's wrong? Are you refusing?"

"I'm refusing."

"Refusing? But why, Donna Noemi?"

"Why? Have you forgotten? I'm old, Efix, and old women don't joke around. Don't talk to me about it any more."

"That's all you have to say?"

"That's all I have to say."

They fell silent. She sewed. He hugged his knees with his clasped hands. He seemed to be dreaming, he didn't understand. Finally he raised his eyes and looked around. No, he wasn't dreaming, it was all real. The courtyard was full of sun and shadows. A piece of wood fell from the balcony like needles fall from pine trees in autumn, and beyond the wall Monte could be seen white as sugar, and everything was as sweet and tender as the morning he left Don Predu's house. He still seemed to hear the women slamming the furniture, but they were blows to his body; yes, something was hitting him on his back, his shoulders, his chest, elbows, knees, knuckles. Pale Donna Noemi was there who sewed and sewed, who stuck his soul with her needle. And the swallows passed continually in circles above their heads like a moving garland of black flowers, of little black crosses. Their shadows ran along the ground like leaves blown by the wind. He remembered the pain he had felt on getting up from below the pulpit and the shadow on the Magdalene's face. He sighed deeply. He understood. It was God's punishment that weighed on him.

Then, slowly, he began to speak, holding on to the hem of Noemi's skirt, and he didn't understand very well what he was saying, but it must not have been very convincing because the woman continued to sew and didn't reply, now calm, with an ambiguous smile on her lips.

Only after he seemed to have gone over everything, all the past miseries, all the splendors to come, did she speak, but in a low tone, barely raising her eyes, almost as if she were speaking only with them.

"Don't worry so much about us, Efix. Don't get involved in our business. And then, you know, we've lived this long; haven't we been all right up to now? Is there anything we don't have? We'll get along with the help of God. We have enough to eat. There is too much stuff in Predu's house and I wouldn't even know how to take care of it."

Efix was thinking desperately. What to do except fall back on a lie?

He began to touch her skirt again.

"I must tell you something very serious, Donna Noemi. I didn't want to, but your stubbornness forces me to. Don Predu is so smitten that if you don't want him he'll die. Yes, it's like he was under a spell, he doesn't sleep any more. You don't know what love is, Donna Noemi. It kills you. It's bad to kill a man...."

Then Noemi laughed and showed all her strong shining teeth like a deliriously happy girl. That laugh irritated Efix so much it made him a wicked liar.

"And then, another thing even more serious, Donna Noemi! Yes, you force me to tell you. Don Giacinto threatens to come back here.... Understand?"

She stopped sewing, straightened up, threw back her head to breathe more easily. Her hands clutched at the cloth.

Efix jumped with fright, believing that she was about to faint.

But it lasted only a moment. She turned to look at him sharply and said calmly, "Even if he comes back there's nothing more to lose. And we don't need anyone to protect us."

He picked the pansy off the ground and went to sit on the stairs, as on the night after Donna Ruth's death. He didn't ask himself anymore why Noemi refused life. He seemed to understand. It was God's punishment of him. The punishment that weighed on the whole house. He was the worm inside the fruit, the termite that gnawed at the family's destiny. Just like the termite he had done everything secretly. He had gnawed, gnawed, gnawed, now was he surprised if everything was crumbling around him? He had to go away. That was all he knew. However a thread of hope still sustained him, like the still fresh stem supported the faded pansy in his hand. God would not abandon the unfortunate women. With him out of the way, perhaps Donna Noemi, offended by the manner of the messenger, would give in. After all, two woman cannot manage alone.

He had to leave. Why hadn't he understood that before? It seemed like a voice was calling him. And a voice really called beyond the wall, from the silence of the road.

He got up and made a move to leave. Then he came back to take the *bisaccia* attached to the peg under the loggia. The peg, there for centuries, came loose and fell in the pebbles of the courtyard like a large black finger. He flinched. Yes, he had to go away. Even the peg came loose to keep from having to hold his *bisaccia* any longer.

And to Noemi's surprise, who had followed his movements out of the corner of her eye, he did not reattach the peg, but walked away.

"Efix? Are you going?"

He stopped, head hanging down.

"You're not waiting for Ester? Are you coming back for Easter?"

He shook his head no.

"Efix, are you angry? Did I say something bad?"

"Nothing bad, *padrona mia*. It's just that I have to go now. It's time."

"Well, then, go on time."

He thought a moment. He seemed to have forgotten something, like when someone gets ready to go on a journey and asks himself if he's thought of everything.

"Donna Noemi, do you want anything?"

"Nothing. Only it seems to me that you aren't feeling well. Are you ill? Stay here, we'll call the doctor. Your legs are trembling."

"I have to go."

"Listen, Efix, don't be hurt by what I said. That's the way it is. I can't, believe me. I know you don't like it, but I can't. Don't say anything to Ester. And go on, if you want to. But if you feel bad, come back. Remember, this house is yours."

He put the *bisaccia* on his shoulders and went out. On the doorsteps he stamped his feet one after the other in order not to carry away even the dust of the house he was leaving.

XIII

Zuannantoni was waiting outside.

"I called you three times. Let's go, grandmother is taken bad and wants to talk to you. Why didn't you come? Don't take your bread out of your *bisaccia*."

The old woman lay still dressed in her bed, as red and hot as blazing kindling. She seemed to be drowsing, but when Efix bent over her she said in a whisper: "You see? She went to the river to wash because she has to work. And you said he would marry her!"

"Zia Pottoi! You have to have patience. We were born to suffer."

The old woman raised her arm and drew him close to her. A putrid, deathly odor rose from the bed; but he didn't move away even when he felt Zia Pottoi's necklace, as hot as if it had been in the fire, graze his face and her breath pass over his hair like a spider.

"Listen, Efix, we are before God. I'm about to leave. Don Zame himself will come get me, just as we agreed when we were children. Now it's time to go away together. And on the road I'll tell him not to stop where he fell, where you killed him, and to forgive you for the love you've had for his daughters. He'll pardon you, Efix. You've carried the weight long enough, but you, you, Efix, for your part save my Grixenda. She's about to be lost. She's only waiting for me to die so she can run away, and I can't close my eyes in peace. Go to the boy and tell him not to let her go, tell him to remember he promised to marry her. And tell him he should marry her, yes, so Donna Noemi won't think about him anymore. Go."

She pushed him away and his eyes widened, feeling as though they were burned, covered with ashes, like he had come back from hell. The old woman didn't reopen her eyes. With her hands rigid, her fingers open, she still moved her violet lips ringed with black, but she wasn't saying anything.

She never spoke again.

A golden ray was raining down on the bed from the hole in the roof, as from an upside down funnel, that illuminated her black body and necklaces, leaving the rest of the desolate room in darkness.

As though from the bottom of a well Efix looked at that high distant point, but suddenly it seemed like the ray deviated so that it rained on him, illuminating him. Everything was clear like this. His eyes now distinguished everything, the dark errors around him, the luminous center that was God's punishment of him.

He took up his *bisaccia* without another word and went away.

Passing by Don Predu's house he called out to Stefana and told her he had to leave on business and didn't know when he'd return.

"At least tell me where you're going."

"To Nuoro."

It took him two days to reach Nuoro. He walked up slowly, with rest stops, throwing himself down at the edge of the road when he was tired. He closed his eyes, but didn't sleep. Opening them again he would see the yellow road lose itself in the green and blue distance, up toward the Nuorese mountains, down toward the sea of Baronia, and it seemed to him that he had always lived this way, on the side of a road, half of the way already finished the other half ahead. Down there he had left the place of his sin, up there, toward the mountain, was the place of his penitence.

The weather was beautiful. The valleys were already grass-covered and the periwinkle were smiling like children's eyes.

Networks of water sparkled among the green of the slopes, and the river murmured among the alder trees. Carts passed on the road, and Efix wanted to ask for a ride, but he immediately dismissed that idea.

No, he had to walk for penitence, to *arrive* without help from anyone.

This first trip had a purpose, however. He was still worried about the things of this world, and about getting rid of them quickly. Afterwards, he felt he would be free, with only his weight to bear patiently until his death.

The first night he stayed in a road keeper's house in the valley, but he couldn't sleep. The night was clear and sweet. In the white sky above the valley enclosed by columns of rocks, the moon hung like a golden lamp from a temple vault. But a sick man groaned in the run-down house, and that human pain disturbed the solitude.

Efix left before dawn, more tired than ever. And there were the mountains of Oliena rising from the white and vaporous darkness like a mass of incense before the rough granite altar of Monte Orthobene. The entire landscape has a holy aspect, and the Redeemer with his cross stops in flight on the highest rock, and flaps his black arms against the golden pallor of the heavens.

Efix knelt down but did not pray, he couldn't pray, he had forgotten the words; but his eyes, his trembling hands, his whole body agitated by fever was a prayer.

The more he walked upwards toward Nuoro the louder he heard something palpitating like a great heart suspended above the valley.

"It's the Mill, and Giacinto's there," he thought joyfully.

It was the last stretch of his worldly journey, the last climb of his calvary, that sloping path, filthy and oily, with a dead cat in the middle of trash, the red sky above high weed covered walls.

Halfway there he turned. A shadow rose from the valley, tracing a brown circle over the rosy peaks of Monte Orthobene, and it reached him also on the path. High above was the panting Mill, a masculine palpitation in contrast to the feminine call of a church bell ringing for vespers. And at the end of the road farmers passed with yoked oxen, powerful burghers like Don Predu, women carrying amphoras on their heads. Some other women sat in pale repose on the low wall that enclosed an exterior courtyard.

Efix began to talk to them, stopped tired in his tracks with his *bisaccia* falling from his shoulders.

"Where is Don Giacinto?"

"Who? The one at the Mill? A little further on. What are you carrying in that *bisaccia*? Are you his servant?"

"Yes. What does Don Giacinto do?"

"Oh, he works and enjoys himself. He's happy. He's a good boy. All the women like him…they fight over him like a honey sweet cake…."

Then Efix remembered the feast of the Rimedio, when Natolia and Grixenda danced together around the stranger; and a burning pain struck him, but with the pain came an intense desire to do something to fend off destiny.

"But where can I find him? Is he at the Mill now?"

"Here he comes!"

In fact, it was Giacinto hurrying along, bareheaded, with his hair and clothes white with flour. Someone had already run to tell him of the servant's arrival.

"What have you come looking for?" he asked, grabbing Efix by the shoulders and giving him a shake.

Efix looked at him without replying and let himself to be dragged down the road as far as a courtyard enclosing two little houses above the valley. A small dwarf-like man, with great melancholy eyes and a white face, was drawing water from the well. Giacinto introduced him as the owner of the house.

"I have to talk to you," Efix said.

"Here I am, talk."

They sat down in the kitchen, but the man was fixing supper and Efix didn't want to talk in his presence. For his part, Giacinto was joking and laughing and didn't try to get him to say anything.

Beyond the little window on the rocks of Monte Orthobene he saw the Redemption statue, small as a swallow, and from the garden wafted the odor of gillyflower, like in the women's courtyard.

Efix felt pain in his heart, but couldn't speak. He only said: "Giacintì, it seems like you're happy now!"

"What should I do? Hang myself?"

But the little man, bending over the cooking macaroni, raised his sad eyes and Giacinto laughed and looked up at the ceiling beams.

"You know, Efix, the first days I came here, as a boarder with this good servant of God, I really tried to hang myself. Remember, Micheli?" The little man nodded yes, but shook his head disapprovingly. "And he saved me, put me to bed like a baby, tied me down to keep me from leaving. I had a high fever. But then it all passed, and now I'm happy and content. Right, Micheli? Aren't I happy and content? Now then, Efix, speak. You surely came to disturb my happiness."

"Old Pottoi is dead," Efix finally said, and Giacinto brought his fork to Efix' face almost as though wanting to poke him.

"Go on, bird of ill omen! I knew you brought news of a death! What else?"

"And Grixenda is getting ready to leave. She'll be here in a few days. That's what I've come to tell you."

Giacinto had the look of a sad and frightened child. "Oh, no, not that! I don't want her to come!"

"You don't want her? How can you stop her? Besides she's your fiancée. You promised to marry her."

"I can't marry her. Isn't that right, Micheli, that I can't? I can't and I don't want to! I'm not in a position to marry. I'm a beggar, I have other duties, you know. Well, then, I can say it in front of this man who knows everything about me, just like you do, and is sorry for me. I have to pay my debt to my aunts. That's why I wanted to die. Because I was desperate. But his man said to me. I'll keep you in my house *for nothing*. I'll give you lodging and food too when I have it, but you must work to pay your debt."

Efix gave the little man a half surprised and a half suspicious look and seemed to ask with his eyes, "why such generosity?" And the man, who was eating with his face bent over his plate, looked up and said: "Because we're Christians!"

Then Efix looked into himself, as into the house of his soul, and remembered why he had come.

"Giacinto, you still have to marry Grixenda. She'll be here in a few days. Don't send her away, don't lose her!"

"But my good man! Can't you hear? I'm telling you I can't take care of her, I can't marry her. I have to pay my debt to my aunts!"

"You'll pay it by marrying her."

"Has she inherited so much?" Giacinto said, laughing. But Efix looked at him seriously, and repeated twice: "I came to talk to you about this."

The owner of the house understood that his presence was too much and he went away silently in spite of Giacinto's urging.

"Let him go," Efix said. "No one must know what I have to tell you."

Even though left alone, they both felt a sense of embarrassment. The light seemed an obstacle between them. They went out to sit in the courtyard. Giacinto pulled the door closed behind him as though to keep the light and fire from hearing, and Efix searched for words to draw the painful secret from his heart. Oh, it seemed too big and heavy to drag out whole: in strips, perhaps yes, bleeding. He bent over himself. He dug deeply, silently, pulling it up like a boulder from a well. Finally, tired and powerless, he looked up with a sigh.

"Giacinto, so I'll tell you. This is the way of the world. Don Predu wants to marry Donna Noemi, but Donna Noemi doesn't want him. It's your fault!"

Giacinto didn't answer, but grabbed his arm tightly as though wanting to pull it off. Then he let him go.

Efix heard him panting slightly, as though taken ill, and with his arm burning Efix's breath came with difficulty.

"Yes, it's your fault, your fault," he began again almost belligerently. "Didn't you know? Finally! At least the old woman didn't tell you this. But now you have to think about it seriously. You've got to remove this worm from your aunt's brain, do you understand? Do you understand?"

"What can *I* do?" Giacinto said finally. And he seemed to have fallen into his old sadness again. Bent over himself in the shadow, he looked at his feet on the ground and saw a dark abyss.

"What can you do? You know, I told you: you begin to do your duty, then she'll do hers...."

"What can I do, what can I do? Do you think we can make our own fate? Remember what we talked about down there at the little farm. Do you remember? Have you made your own destiny?"

Efix also bent over. He remained like that, close, so close that each felt the heat from the other. They stayed almost temple to temple, as though listening to a voice from underground.

"It's true! We can't make our fate," Efix admitted.

"And then, you think she would be happy marrying Zio Pietro? Bread's not enough to make us happy; even I understand that now.... It takes more than that!"

"But you, tell me...you...."

"Me?"

"Yes, you, did you know?"

"What do you want me to say? A man always notices these things. But I swear to you on my mother's soul, I've always respected Noemi, like a holy thing.... And yet, yes, I'll tell you, because I know that I can tell you, only once, when she fainted and I cried over her, yes, I can tell you like I could tell my mother, with the same innocence, yes, we looked at each other…through our tears, and perhaps then…perhaps then.… I don't know. That's all I'll say. Maybe that's why I went away, more than for the wrong I've done."

"Let me ask you something else. When you came to the farm, the last time, did you already know?"

"I already knew."

"Well, then," Efix said as he rose, "you are a man!"

"What do you expect?" Giacinto replied, feeling flattered. "I know a little about life, not much. You learn about life quickly where I was born. But you've learned about life in your own way, and so we understand each other even if we don't speak the same language. Remember when I came to the farm.… I gambled and faked the signature because I wanted to pay the Captain what I owed him and make a good impression when I went back. He would have said: that poor boy turned out all right. Instead of that I went down, down.… It was like I'd lost my mind: but now I've opened my eyes and see where my true salvation lies. Where have you found your true salvation? Living for others. I want to do the same, Efix."

Speaking right into his face, Giacinto added, "You've saved me. I want to be like you.… Tell me, am I right? I threw you on the ground at Oliena, but even saints have been mistreated, and that didn't keep them from being saints. Tell me, am I right?" he repeated shaking him by the shoulders. "Remember the things we said at the farm? I'll always remember them, and in fact I say to myself: Efix and I are two unlucky men, but we're both men, more than Zio Pietro, more than Milese, that's for sure! Zio Pietro? What's Zio Pietro? He let his cousins suffer alone for so many years in poverty, mocked by the whole town. And now he thinks he's doing good because he wants to marry Noemi! He's doing it because he likes her as a woman, like I like Grixenda, nothing more. Is that love, is it charity? She's right not to want him. She's right! I'm on her side! You're the only one who has really loved them. And if one of them wanted to love and get married, I say it should be you and not Zio

Pietro. Instead they kicked you out like an old dog, now that you aren't good for anything any more. And yet you love them even more because your heart is a real man's heart. Well, now, what are you doing? Hey!... Shame on you! Haven't you cried enough? Come on, be a man! Get hold of yourself."

He shook him again, grabbing him by the shoulders from behind. Efix had doubled over crying, with his head between his knees, his moan filling the silence of the night. He was remembering the blood he had vomited in front of the old church at Oliena, after the other scene with Giacinto. Now it seemed to him that all his blood was pouring from his eyes: all bad blood, the blood of sin. His body was exhausted by it, and his soul was battered inside a space as empty and black as night; but Giacinto's words of love brightened the dark depths, illuminated by his tears shining like stars.

Efix remained in Nuoro for one week.

Both he and Giacinto expected to see Grixenda arrive from one moment to the next, but the days went by and she did not come.

Giacinto had not yet made a decision about it, but seemed calm. He worked, he returned home only during the dinner hour and joked with his landlord, asking his advice about what he should say to his girlfriend.

"I certainly don't want to lose her, poor orphan! What if we married and stayed with you? You need a woman in the house."

The little man looked at him critically but didn't speak, at least in Efix' presence. As far as Efix was concerned, he didn't want to tempt fate, and believed it a sin to try to oppose providence. One needed to give oneself over to it, like a seed in the wind. God knows what He's doing.

In the meantime Efix hadn't made up his mind to leave, waiting for Grixenda. When Giacinto was not in the house he would go down the lane, sit on the brow of the valley and watch the white road at the foot of Monte Orthobene. The palpitating Mill affected him deeply. It seemed like a beating heart, a new heart that rejuvenated the ancient wild land. Inside that palpitation beat Giacinto's blood, and Efix felt like weeping thinking of him. He seemed to see him, tall, serene, white with flour like a young plant covered with hoar frost, purified by work and good intentions. Everyone loved him and he was good to everyone. The women who brought grain to the Mill gathered around him stooped over to weigh the flour, and they looked at him with a mother's eyes, with eyes of love. Efix had gone there one evening, and between the pounding of the machine and the movement of the shadows and the screech of the weights, he seemed to be looking on a scene of Purgatory, and Giacinto suffering among the damned, but waiting for his expiation to end.

The Sunday after Easter Efix went to a country festival at the little church of Valverde.

It was a cold afternoon and winter still seemed to be in charge over the Isalle valley beaten by the northern wind, with Monte Albo in the clouds in the background, like a ship caught in a stormy sea.

Efix followed a column of townsmen wrapped in heavy coats, and with the wind battering his chest he felt something new, strong, penetrate his heart. People were walking, sad but calm, as in a procession, heading not toward a place of festivity but of prayer. An accordion in the distance repeated the religious motif of the sacred lauds, and he felt his penitence had begun.

After he reached the church on the crest of the rocky hill, he sat down by the door and began to pray. It seemed to him that the little Madonna looking out from her damp niche was a little frightened of the people coming to disturb her solitude, and that the wind blew hard and the sun fell quickly over the valley to drive the intruders away. In fact the women wrapped themselves more tightly in their shawls and started home after reciting the rosary.

Only a vender of torrone and black flour dolls covered with sugar stayed, along with two men who sat on either side of the church door under the crumbling atrium.

Efix sat a little distance away, watching them gravely. He recognized them, having seen them at the Feast of the Rimedio. They were both beggars, dressed well enough in blue trousers and fustian jackets. One of them – still young, tall and bent, with a thin yellow face that seemed skin over bones, his purple eyelids lowered – was begging, hardly moving his gray lips over his large protruding teeth, as though he were dreaming and talking in his sleep, indifferent to the exterior world. The other – old but strong, with a ruddy face, shaking all over – had put his cap between his open legs and from time to time bent over to look at the few coins.

The evening fell swiftly, heavy with clouds, and the people went away. The candy vendor closed her still-full boxes and began complaining to the beggars.

"It's not worth the trouble to come so far! An unimportant festival, my brothers!"

"You can't make a living any more," said the old beggar, pouring the coins in a handkerchief and putting his cap on his head. But he fell as he tried to get up, his feet slipping on the stones at the church entrance, and his head and hands hit the ground.

At the clink of coins against the stones the other beggar raised his ashen face, opening his glassy eyes wide as though hearing a threatening sound.

The old man moaned. The woman and Efix ran over to him, but couldn't get him to hold his head up.

"We've got to get him to lie down," the woman said. "I'll give him a little liquor. Put him down. Help me."

He was lying down, but the drops of a green liquid that she tried to pour in his mouth spread over his chin.

"He looks dead. And you, can't you do anything?" she said to the other beggar. "Was he sick? Can't you answer?"

The man tried to talk, but only a tremulous whimper came out of his mouth. Then he broke into tears.

"Get up, move, go get the shepherds down there in the woods."

"Where are you sending a blind man?" Efix said, kneeling with one hand on the old man's heart. The heart jumped as though trying to beat regularly, but each time subsided.

Shadows thickened quickly. Every cloud passing over the horizon left a veil, the wind howled behind the church. The low scrub, a luminous metallic green agitated by a convulsion of sadness and terror, leaned toward the valley trembling like it wanted to escape.

Even the woman was afraid of the solitude and that sudden dying. She put the boxes on her head and said: "I have to go. I'll tell the doctor at Nuoro.

And so Efix remained alone with a dying man and a blind man.

"My companion suffers from heart trouble," the beggar said. "These past days he's felt bad. But no one believed him. People never believe him."

"Are you relatives?"

"No. We met ten years ago at the *Festa del miracolo*. I had a companion then, Juanne Maria, who treated me like a dog. Then this poor man took me with him. He treated me like a son. He never let go of my hand before I was safely seated. Now it's all over."

"What will you do?"

"What can I do? I'll stay here and wait for death. I have everything I own with me, God help me."

"I can take you as far as Nuoro," Efix said, and suddenly he began to cry.

Bending over the dying man he tried to revive him by bathing his lips with the liquor the woman left and dabbing his forehead with a rag dipped in wine. But the man's tragic face was violet and green, growing harder and more immobile in the twilight gloom. His heart stopped beating. Efix relived the most terrible moment of his life. He remembered the bridge, down there, in the reeds undulating in the moonlight, when he bent over to listen to the heart of his dead master.

And yet he felt relieved, like one who finds his way, his point of departure, after wandering lost in impenetrable regions.

"Aren't you going?" the blind man asked without moving.

"I'll go when God commands. Right now I'll light a fire because we have to spend the night here."

He went in search of firewood. The wind blew harder and clouds rose and fell over Monte Orthobene, up and down like a torrent of lava, like columns of smoke, spreading over the whole valley. But high over Nuoro a streak of sad blue lapis lazuli sky remained and the rosy new moon went down between two cliffs.

When he came back Efix saw the blind man had moved and was bent over his companion, calling him by name. He was crying and looking for the money. When he found it he slipped it into his shirt and continued weeping.

And so they spent the night. The blind man told of his misfortunes, alternating that with Bible stories, and his sorrow was calmed, like a violent illness that soon passes.

"What do you think, brother? I was born rich, my father was like Jacob, but without so many children, and he used to say: it's not important if my son is blind, his eyes are gold (referring to his wealth) and he'll see just the same. And my mother who I remember had a voice as sweet as fruit, said: just as long as my Istène keeps his innocence, nothing else is important. And so I tell you, brother, they took everything when my father and mother died. They picked me like a bunch of grapes, everyone, relatives and acquaintances, God forgive them. They forced me to go begging, but I kept my innocence, and so I tell you: I've never wronged anyone. The Lord has always helped me: first Juanne Maria, God keep him in glory, then this one, have been my companions, my brothers, like the angels that accompanied Tobias. Now...."

"Even now you have company," Efix said gravely. "But what do you mean when you say you're innocent?"

"That I'm walking toward eternity," the blind man said quietly. "I'm going toward a door that will open wide for me, and that's all I think about. If I have bread I eat it, if not I keep quiet. I've never touched anyone else's things. I've never known a woman. Juanne Maria once brought one to me. I smelled the odor of evil and threw myself on the ground like the wind. What should I do? If I don't save my soul what would I have, brother?"

"But you took this dying man's money, you scoundrel!" Efix said.

"It was mine. What good's money to a dead man? So I tell you, no, I've never robbed or spilled blood. Not even Joseph's brothers spilled blood. Jude said to them: better to sell him to the Israelites than kill him. And so they did. Do you know the whole story of Joseph the Jew? I'm sorry you're leaving; otherwise I'd tell you."

"No, I'm not going," Efix said. "I'll stay with you from now on. We'll take care of each other."

The blind man lowered his head for a moment, touching the money wrapped in a handkerchief. He didn't appear to be surprised by the decision taken by the stranger. He only asked: "Are you a beggar, too?"

"Yes," Efix said. "Didn't you realize that?"

"Then it's all right. You keep it." And he handed Efix the money.

XIV

From there they went to the *Festa dello Santo Spirito*. The blind man knew the date of every church festival and the itinerary to follow, and it was he who guided his companion.

Passing through Nuoro Efix led him to the Mill, leaned him against a wall, and went to see Giacinto.

"I'm leaving today for far away places. *Addio*. Remember your promise."

Giacinto was weighing a sack of ground barley. He looked up with his eyelids white with flour and smiled. "What promise?"

"To weigh well," Efix said and left.

Once the sack was weighed, Giacinto went outside and saw the two beggars walking away, holding onto each other's pale and trembling hands like two sick men. He called, but Efix only made a gesture of farewell without turning.

Barely outside the town they began quarreling, because even though the blind man had a full *bisaccia*, he wanted to ask for handouts from the passersby, while Efix observed: "Why beg if we don't need to?"

"And tomorrow? Don't you think about tomorrow? What kind of beggar are you? I can see you are new at it."

Then Efix realized that he didn't want to beg because he was ashamed, and his shame made him blush.

The weather had turned nasty. Toward evening it began to rain and the two companions went to a shepherd's hut. But they weren't welcome inside, and so had to take shelter under a roof of branches next to the herd. Dogs barked, a sad misty veil surrounded the whole damp plain, and the little fire that Efix tried to light sputtered in the rain and wind.

The blind man remained impassive, stock-still behind his sorrowful mask. Seated – he never lay down – with his arms around his knees, with his large yellow teeth shining in the fire's reflection, his violet eyelids lowered, he continued telling stories.

"You must know that it took thirteen long years to build King Solomon's house. It was in a woods called Lebanon, named for the tall cedars that grew there. A cool place. And the whole house was made of gold and silver pillars, and carved ceiling beams, and marble floors like in churches. In the middle of the house was a courtyard with a fountain that ran day and night, and the walls were made of fine rocks, cut into equal pieces like bricks. You couldn't count the riches that were inside. The plates and vases were gold, and the whole house was decorated with golden pomegranates and lilies. Even the dogs' collars were gold and the horses' harness silver and the blankets were scarlet. The Queen of Sheba came. She had heard stories of these things from the other end of the world, and was jealous because she was rich, too, and wanted to see who was richer. Women are curious...."

Attracted by the blind man's stories, one of the shepherds came to the shed and bent over to keep dry. His companions followed him.

Excited by his success the blind man became animated. He sat up and told the story of Tamara and the fritters. The shepherds laughed, poking each other with their elbows. They brought milk and bread and gave the blind man money.

Efix was sad, and as soon as they were alone his companion shouted at him for his bad example.

"You talk like my mother," the blind man said, and he went to sleep under the rain.

At the *Festa dello Santo Spirito* there were few people, but well-to-do: rich shepherds with fat wives and beautiful slender daughters. They arrived on horseback. The men proud and dark, with long knives stuck in scabbards of incised leather on their belts, the young men tall, with their teeth and whites of their eyes sparkling, nimble as Bedouins. The girls were willowy, sweet as the biblical figures evoked by the blind man.

The weather was foggy, and enveloping the brown church amid the rocks and thickets of the plain was an infinite silence, a harsh woodland odor. The racing clouds in the gray sky gave an even more fantastic aspect to the place.

All morning men on horseback emerged from the misty path and dismounted silently, as for a secret meeting at that point far from the world. Efix sitting with the blind man at the church entrance felt like he was dreaming.

There were no other beggars here, either, and he felt a vague sense of fear when the strong, proud men, from whose mouths and nostrils issued a vapor of life, passed before him: a sense of fear and shame and even envy. These were men. Their hands looked like claws ready to grab fortune on the wing. They all looked like bandits, above the law, never sorry for their sins if they had any, not tormented for having made their own justice in life. Efix thought they looked at him scornfully as they threw him money, that they were ashamed of him as a man and were ready to nudge him out of their way with their foot like a dirty rag.

But then he looked off into the distance. Another world seemed to begin beyond the fog, and the door open that the blind man spoke of: the great gate of eternity. And he was sorry for his shame.

At his side his companion continued to beg aloud for charity, or to turn to him so the passersby could hear him: "What do we do in this life as important as the pious who give us charity?"

"What do we do, dear brother?"

"Well, my companion, everything happens according to the Lord. We are instruments and he uses us to test men's hearts, like the farmer uses the hoe to move the earth and see if it is fertile. Men, don't look at us as two poor creatures, poorer than fallen leaves, filthier than lepers. Look at us as instruments of the Lord to move your hearts!"

Copper coins fell like hard metallic flowers. Two handsome young Nuorese began to throw money at the blind man to make the girls notice them, aiming at his chest from a distance and laughing every time they hit him. Then they came closer and aimed at Efix, enjoying him as a target. Efix started at every blow and felt like they were stoning him, but he gathered up the coins with a certain eagerness, and then finally, when the game was over, he felt regret and shame once more.

In the meantime the women prepared dinner. They had lit a fire under the solitary tree and smoke mixed with the fog. Their red bodices stood out against the gray livelier than the flame. There were neither songs nor music at this little festival that to Efix seemed like a meeting of bandits and shepherds gathered there out of desire to see their women again and listen to the holy mass.

At midday everyone gathered under the tree around the fire, with the priest sitting in the middle of them. The weather cleared, a golden sun ray at the zenith filtered through the clouds and fell on the banquet tree. Underneath the tree shepherds sitting on the ground, women with baskets in their hands, the priest with a *bisaccia* tossed over his shoulders like a shawl to protect himself from the dampness, laughing children, dogs wagging their tails and watching their masters closely in expectation of a bone to gnaw, everything recalling the sweet serenity of a biblical scene.

Pious women brought large dishes of meat and bread to the two beggars, and when he heard the rustling of their steps on the grass the blind man raised his voice and began to tell a story.

"Yes, once there was a king who had his people worship trees and animals, and even fire. God was offended and made this king's servants turn so bad they plotted to kill their master. And so they did. Yes, he made them worship a golden God. This is why there is so much love for money in the world, and even relatives kill relatives for money. It happened to me. My relatives, because I was blind, stripped me like the wind strips a tree in autumn."

Everyone soon left, and the two men remained alone once more in the gloom of the deserted place.

The fog thinned. The black woods appeared profiled against the pale blue horizon. Then everything became serene, as if invisible hands had drawn back the veil of bad weather, and a large rainbow with seven vivid colors and another smaller, paler one curved over the countryside. The Nuorese spring smiled on poor Efix sitting by the door of the little church. Large yellow buttercups, damp as though with dew, shone in the silvery meadows, and the first stars appearing at sunset smiled down at the flowers. Sky and land seemed like two mirrors reflecting each other.

A nightingale sang in the solitary tree still permeated with smoke. All the freshness of evening, all the harmony of the serene distance, and the stars smiling at the flowers and the flowers smiling at the stars, and the proud joy of handsome young shepherds and the repressed passion of women in red bodices, and all the melancholy of the poor who live waiting for leftovers from the tables of the rich, and the distant sorrows and hopes, and the past, the lost country, love, sin, remorse, prayer, the hymn of the pilgrim who travels far not knowing where he'll spend the night, but he feels guided by God, and the green solitude of the little farm down there, the voice of the river and alder trees there, the odor of euphorbia, Grixenda's laughter and tears, Noemi's laughter and tears, Efix's laughter and tears, the whole world's laughter and tears, trembled and vibrated in the notes of the nightingale above in the solitary tree that seemed higher than the mountains, with its top touching the sky and the tip of the highest leaf stuck in a star.

Efix began crying again. He didn't know why, but he was crying. He felt all alone in the world, with the nightingale for company.

He could still feel the coins of the young Nuorese hitting his chest, and he jumped as if they were stoning him; but it was a shudder of joy, the delight of martyrdom.

His companion, with his back against the closed door and his hands around his knees, snored as he slept.

From there they went to Fonni for the *Festa dei Santi Martiri*. They always broke their walk into short intervals, stopping at sheepfolds where the blind man would get shepherds to listen to him. He seemed to recognize them "by the smell," he said, recounting the more emotional episodes of the Old Testament for the more simple and God-fearing men. Those episodes interpreting evil had a prurient flavor for young men and libertines.

His companion's behavior saddened Efix. At times he felt so sickened by it that he considered leaving him, but on thinking it over it seemed his penance was more complete this way, and he said to himself: "It's like leading a sick man, a leper. God will give me more credit for my work of mercy."

Other beggars going to the festival joined them on the road. Everyone greeted the blind man like an old acquaintance, but looked at Efix suspiciously.

"You're still strong and able," a young man said to him. "Why are you asking for charity?"

"I have a secret disease that consumes me and keeps me from working," Efix answered, ashamed of his lie. "God commands us to work as long as we can. If only I could work! Oh, how happy are those who can work!"

Efix was thinking of Giacinto, happy and good after finding work, and he asked himself sorrowfully if he hadn't made a mistake by leaving the poor Pintor women.

And so he continued traveling, but he didn't find peace, and his thoughts were always down there, among the reeds and alder trees of the little farm. If a nightingale sang, especially in the evenings, he would be tormented by yearning.

"What will Don Predu think, who's waiting for me to give him Noemi's answer? God will provide. And he'll provide well, now that I'm far from *them* with my mortal sin and my excommunication."

And he continued traveling with the beggars up across the green valley of Mamojada, up toward Fonni on paths over which loomed the mountains of Gennargentu, with fantastic forms on cloudy evenings of ramparts, castles, Cyclopean tombs, silver cities, blue woods covered with fog. But his body seemed like an empty sack to him, battered by the wind, torn, dirty, good only for tossing on the rag heap.

And his companions were not good company. They didn't know where they were going, they didn't know why. They weren't interested in the entertainment in the places where they went, considering them neither happier nor sadder than the lonely places where they stopped to rest or eat.

Yet they quarreled among themselves, shouted obscenities, took God's name in vain, were envious of each other. They had all the emotions of more fortunate men. Efix, dead tired, feverish to his bones, didn't try to convert them, or even feel pity for them, but he seemed to be walking in a dream, carried away by a group of phantoms, like so many nights at the farm. He was already dead and still wandering through the world, driven out of those kingdoms.

At Fonni, where the beggars gathered in the courtyard around the Basilica full of people from distant towns, he began to feel a new torment. He was afraid of being recognized, and tried to hide behind his companion.

Two other beggars were with them, an old blind man and a young man who, before he arrived, had pricked a spot under his right breast and rubbed a poisonous grass on it to make it swell. He then exhibited it to the crowd as a malignant tumor.

Efix was angry about this deception, and when coins fell into his companion's cap he blushed, feeling like he too had deceived the pious.

And the coins kept falling. He had never imagined that there were so many charitable people in the world. The women were especially generous, and a sweet shadow veiled their eyes every time the young beggar's tumor appeared, swollen and dark as a fig in the folds of his open shirt.

Almost every woman stopped, bent over to look questioningly. Some were tall, slender, wrapped in orbace, with aprons embroidered with yellow and green hieroglyphs and scarlet hoods that seemed to have come from another region, from ancient Egypt. Others had powerful hips, wide faces with two red apple cheeks, fleshy lips, ardent and moist like the rim of a honey jar.

Efix responded to their questions with downcast eyes, and sadly collected the alms.

But some men also stopped by the old blind man and the fake sick man, and one bent over to get a good look at the tumor.

"Yes, God help me," he said. "It's true. He has only a year to live."

"Only a year?" shouted another man. "Oh, that's not enough to finish even three of the thousand things I'm thinking of doing. Here, take it!"

He threw a silver coin at the sick man. Then it was a contest who could offer more to the man condemned to die soon. Coins rained upon his *bisaccia*, so many that Efix's companion went livid and his voice trembled from envy. At noon he refused to eat. Then he fell silent and seemed to be plotting something ominous. In fact, when the crowd gathered again in the courtyard and the women dug in their pockets to give alms to the fake, he began to shout:

"Look at him carefully! He's as healthy as you are. He stuck himself with a poisoned needle."

Then someone bent over to get a better look at the fake tumor, but the beggar, pale and still, didn't react, didn't speak; however, his old companion suddenly got up, tall, wavering like a tree trunk shaken by the wind. He took a few steps and pulled Istène down, pounding on his head with his fists like two hammers.

At first Istène bowed his head nearly to his knees; then he sat up, seized the legs of his assailant and shook him hard, and being unable to bring him down, bit him on the knee. They didn't speak and their silence made the scene more tragic. After a moment, however, people gathered around them, and the women's shrieks joined with the men's laughter.

"I'd like to know how he saw it!"

"If he's not blind! Damn them all, they're pretending from start to finish."

"And I gave him nine reali three times! How did you make the tumor?... Tell me and I'll give you nine more. I want to do the same thing to keep out of the army."

"Watch out, the soldiers are coming."

"Everyone be quiet. It's nothing."

The people separated to let the *carabinieri* pass. Tall, with red and blue plumes fluttering like a fantastic bird, they stood over the two beggars curled up on the ground.

The old man trembled with rage, but didn't open his mouth. The other one was sitting up again and said in a sad voice that he didn't know anything, that he hadn't moved, that he'd felt a man fall on him like a collapsing wall.

The *carabinieri* made them get up and go with them. The crowd followed behind as in a procession. Efix followed too, but his legs were trembling and a veil covered his eyes.

"Now they'll arrest me too and want to know who I am and everything about me, and I'll be condemned."

But no one paid any attention to him, and after the two blind men were inside the barracks the people went away and Efix remained alone in the distance, sitting on a rock, waiting.

He was afraid, but he wouldn't have abandoned the blind man for anything in the world. He stayed there an hour, then two, three. The place was silent. People were down at the festival and that corner of the village seemed uninhabited. The sun beat on the roofs of the houses low and humble as huts. The afternoon wind carried the smell of aromatic grasses and distant shouts and music.

That peace increased Efix's agitation. For the first time the error of his penance seemed clear to him, like the rock there on the mountains seen through the diaphanous air. No, this was not what he had dreamed.

And what about his poor *padrone* suffering, alone, abandoned? For the first time he considered returning, finishing his days at their feet like a faithful dog. To return, even to condemn his soul, but not to let them suffer. This was his true penance. But he couldn't abandon his companion. Just then the barracks' door opened and the two blind men came out holding each others' hands like brothers.

Efix went up to meet them and took his companion by his hand. Thus in a row they returned to the courtyard of the Basilica, and went around looking for the man who pretended to be ill. People were dancing and playing music, the sunset colored the bell tower, roofs, trees red. From the church came psalms of praise that accompanied the dance music, and the perfume of incense mixed with the odor from the orchard.

However, as hard as they looked, the fake sick man was not to be found either in the courtyard or the church, or even in the streets. Some said he had run away out of fear of the *carabinieri*. And so Efix remained with the two blind men.

XV

Efix pulled the blind men behind him for quite a while.

They went from festival to festival, alone or with other beggars, like condemned men going to an unreachable place of punishment.

The feasts were very much alike. The important ones were in spring and fall, and took place around solitary little rural churches in the mountains, on the high plains, at the edge of valleys. Then it was like a sudden reflowering, an eruption of life and joy in a place deserted all year long, in wild and uncultivated fields. The colorful costumes – red bodices, yellow bands, bright crimson aprons – would gleam like colorful flowers among green of the mastic trees and the ivory-colored stubble.

And everywhere they drank, sang, danced, laughed.

Efix, dressed like the other beggars, came with the two blind men behind him, and they seemed his destiny: his sin and his punishment. He didn't love them, but he tolerated them with infinite patience.

They didn't love him either, but they vied with each other for his attention, and quarreled endlessly.

August and September were the busiest, an exhausting series of festivals. First they went up Monte Orthobene for the *Festa del Redentore* in August. A large red moon rose from the sea and illuminated the woods. From there Efix saw his Monte far off in the distance. He spent the night praying under the Redeemer statue with its black cross that seemed to join blue sky to gray land. At dawn he heard distant singing. A procession came up from the valley and in a moment the rocks were covered with white and red, the shrubs flowered with faces of smiling children, and under the holm oaks old shepherds kneeled down like converted Druids.

On the hewn stone altar the chalice gleamed in the sun, and the Redeemer seemed to pause before taking flight from the rock. Someone was crying loudly. It was a beggar between two blind men behind a bush. It was Efix.

In September they climbed up Mount Gonare. The weather turned bad again, wracked by violent storms. Rivulets of muddy water furrowed the slopes in wind-twisted woods, and the whole mountain quaked with thunder. The faithful came anyway. They came up by torturous paths, by all the winding roads, flowing into the little church like blood goes up through veins to the heart.

From a stone niche where he had taken shelter with his companions, Efix saw figures passing through the fog like clouds, and the story of the Universal Flood that the young blind man told seemed their story. And here came some surviving patriarchs to take refuge on Mount Gonare. They came with their women and children, and were both happy and sad because they had lost everything and saved everything.

The women especially looked down from the height of their horses, from the frame of their kerchiefs, with large dismayed eyes suddenly sparkling with joy: something frightened them, something gladdened them, perhaps their fear itself. And distant shouts in the fog sounded like whinnies of wild horses running in the wind.

Efix was always afraid of being recognized even though he was wearing a suit and a shaggy gray beard like a half mask made of donkey hair. He watched the figures passing on the path in front of him to see if anyone noticed him, and in fact all of a sudden he squatted down, closing his eyes like children do when they want to hide.

One man, lolling on his black horse, slowly rode up, covered by an orbace cloak lined in scarlet. The wind lifted the hem of his Spanish-style cloak and revealed the rider's embroidered *bisaccia* and large legs with spurs shining like silver. His hood shaded a good-natured, cynical face that was turned toward the beggars, and he sneered slightly as he tossed them some coins.

Efix opened his eyes and slowly looked up.

"Do you know who that man is?" he said to the young blind man. "He's my *padrone*!"

After the rain stopped, the three companions continued climbing, silent, bent. Clouds scuttled above the rocks, shrubs and wind-twisted trees that were crazy with the desire to tear themselves from earth and follow them. The thunder continued crashing. Everything was full of turbulence and anxiety, and Efix felt himself swept like a dry leaf in the tumult.

They took a place next to one of the crosses on the path.

The wind blew continuously, but later the sun appeared among the clouds and pushed them to the horizon, and everything sparkled around the mountains and valleys where the fog had collected in luminous silvery lakes.

The beggars were warmed by the sun, and Efix collected the alms, trembling at every footstep for fear of seeing Don Predu again. However, from time to time he raised his head as though listening to a far off voice.

He felt like he was still sitting in front of his hut on the farm listening to the reeds rustling, and the voice of his heart said: "Efix, if are you staying here for penance why are you afraid of being recognized? Get up when your *padrone* goes by and greet him."

Suddenly a sense of joy made him jump, it penetrated everything like the sun that dried his clothes and warmed his stiff limbs. He thought again of the women he still loved, and waited for Don Predu to ask for news of them.

However, Don Predu did not come back down.

After hearing mass a group of young town girls as beautiful as roses came down one after the other, laughing.

"Did you see that big man in church?" one of them asked. "He's a very rich nobleman under a spell."

"Yes, I know. A poor woman he was supposed to marry and didn't had him bewitched."

"Go hang yourself, Maria, what are you saying? If she put a spell on him it was to get him to marry her...."

"Go break your neck. Don't give me a hard time, Franzisca Bè!"

With teeth gleaming in a beautiful mouth full of bad words, they passed by Efix. One of them stopped to throw a coin to the beggars and the wind raised the edge of her embroidered kerchief.

Efix was waiting for Don Predu. The patriarchs descended the path: taciturn women, young men with supple legs, little shepherds with eyes sad with solitude. Don Predu was not to be seen.

Efix kept waiting. After midday everyone had already returned to the cabins down in the glade, and Don Predu still had not come by.

Then Efix helped his companions climb up as far as the little church. In front of it were only a few young men clinging to the side of the cliff to watch some barb horses run. There, half way down the slope, the long horses mounted by hooded townsmen seemed to be carried by the wind.

Efix settled the blind men against the wall while he went into the church, going along on tip toe up to the altar steps where Don Predu was on his knees praying with upraised face, his bluish hair in the shadows gilded by candles, the red hem of his cloak turned back, spurs on his feet, similar in every way to the Barons on a pilgrimage that the servant had seen in some old paintings of the Basilica.

He was absorbed in prayer, but when Efix touched his hood lightly he turned, first surprised, and then angry, without recognizing the beggar.

"Go to the devil! Can't you leave anyone in peace even here?"

"Don Predu! I'm Efix, don't you recognize me?"

Don Predu jumped up, raising the hems of his cloak almost as though to embrace his servant. They looked at each other like two old friends.

"Well, then? Well, then?"

"Well, then?

"Yes," Don Predu said, the first to recover. "Giacinto told me about your exploits, old fellow. Now, you've taken up an easy occupation, you old lazy bones! A fine occupation, yes, indeed! Here, take it!"

He held out a coin, but Efix looked him in the eye with his eyes of a faithful dog and sighed but didn't take offense.

"Don Predu, give me news of my *padrone*."

"Your *padrone*? Who sees them? They stay closed up in their den like martens."

"And Giacinto?"

"I saw that good for nothing at Nuoro. Why didn't you take him begging with you? And do you know what he's doing now? That stupid boy is marrying that other good for nothing, Grixenda!"

"That's good. He promised he would," Efix said, and again he was filled with joy. "There's the grace you were asking for," he was thinking, and smiled at the insults that Don Predu, regretting his first impulse of benevolence, turned on him, treating him like the beggar he was.

After the feast of San Cosma and Damiano at Mamojada, Efix and the blind men went to Bitti for the feast of the *Madonna del Miracolo*. Before reaching Bitti they stopped above Orune, but even though Efix was tired he couldn't sleep for fear that they would rob his *bisaccia* with its hoard collected at other festivals. He prayed quietly, opening his eyes occasionally to look at his companions asleep under an oak tree.

It was still night, but a sliver of light came between the mountains to the east that opened toward the sea. Dawn was waking down there. And here Efix, overcome by sleep, believed he could no longer lift his eyelids and was dreaming.

He saw the old blind man sit down, listen attentively, lean a hand on the trunk of the oak, get up, and after a moment's hesitation come over to him, and with his hand as a hook he drew up his *bisaccia* as though fishing it out of the shadows.

Efix didn't move or speak, and the old man went away quietly, up through the thicket and rocks without turning, large and black against the blue background of the mountain.

Only when Efix could no longer see him did he realize he hadn't been dreaming, and he jumped to his feet, but it seemed as though a hand pulled him down, forcing him to sit again, to stay motionless. And gradually surprise turned to joy, an impulse to laugh. And he laughed, and all around the sky turned blue and pink, and the birds sang in the brush.

"God has freed me of one of my companions," he thought. "Oh, what a weight has been removed!"

He woke the other man and told him what happened.

"You see? Efix, now are you convinced? I knew he was pretending. Didn't I say that from the beginning? And you brought him along. You tormented me day and night with him. Now let's go report him. We'll look for him. We'll stomp his bones."

Efix smiled. During the festival he was almost happy. A crowd unlike any he had seen before filled the church, the fields around, the path that led to town. A procession went continually around the sanctuary like a red and white, yellow and black snake. Standards waved like large butterflies. Choral chants, the jingling of the bard horses harnessed for the race, shouts of joy united with the pilgrims' solemn songs. Women went by with their black hair loose on their shoulders like mourning veils; men followed with uncovered heads, candles in hand, barefoot, dusty as though they had come from the other end of the world. All eyes were full of wonder and hope.

The patient horses, loaded with joy and sorrow, climbed up the path. Riding them were young men with flaming faces, swollen with blood; pale young women that hid their passion like embers under ashes; and the infirm, crazy, possessed. All eyes were full of life and death.

Efix was a little distance from the church in a place where few people passed. The blind man continued to complain, going from one lamentation to another, and he had a gloomy, menacing face.

Toward evening – the collection had been sparse – he gave vent to his spleen, accusing Efix of having killed the other companion to free himself and to keep the money.

Efix smiled. "Come," he said, putting out his hand, and after having walked a little: "Do you hear?"

The blind man heard the voice of the other companion who was there in front of them begging for charity.

"Now don't do like you did the other time," Efix said. "If you get into a fight and they arrest you, I'll wash my hands of you, I swear."

Then the real blind man bent over the fake blind man and asked him quietly, through clenched teeth: "Why have you done this, you Pharisee?"

"Just because I felt like it."

Efix smiled. The blind man *saw* this smile and was exasperated by it. All his anger for the other thief was turned on his good companion. "I don't want to go with you any longer. I'd rather throw myself down and die. You are stupid, a good for nothing. You came with me to amuse yourself and torment me. Go to hell."

"You talk like that because you know I'll never leave you," Efix replied. "You know me even though you're blind, and I don't know you even though I can see. But if you think you can find another companion, go ahead. I'll help you."

The fake blind man was listening, with the stolen *bisaccia* close by. He held out a hand to Istène and said: "Then stay with me, devil!"

They remained like that, holding hands like they had when they came out of the barracks at Fonni, and it seemed like they were waiting for him to say something, challenging him. In response Efix took out the money collected that day, and after dangling it in front of them and looking at them with a smile, he let it fall into the real blind man's hand and went away.

Free! Yet he had the physical impression he was still dragging his companions behind him, and that kept them on his mind.

He walked all night and all the next day, down along the Isalle valley until he reached the sea. There he threw himself on the ground between two phillyrea bushes, and he felt like he had just returned from a trip around the world.

But in his sleep he saw the blind man bend over him, with his livid lips half opened over his wild-animal teeth, and it seemed he was both mocking and pitying him.

"You think you've come back to rest. You'll see, Efix; now your journey is really just beginning."

Climbing up the wide road, the closer he got to the farm the louder grew a accordion's lament. It seemed like a trick of his ears accustomed to the festival music.

So many things from the past came back to mind. And all the leaves shook a greeting to him. Here was the hedge, there the river, the hill, the hut. He wasn't excited, but that sweet, veiled lament that seemed to rise out of the quiet green water drew him like a magnet.

As he walked up and looked around he realized that the farm was badly cared for. It looked like a place with no owner. The trees were nearly bare of fruit and broken limbs hung askew.

Zuannantoni, sitting under the pergola in front of the hut, was playing the accordion; and the monotonous theme spread over everything like a veil of sleep over the desolate place.

When he saw the stranger come up and bend over to look into the hut, the boy stopped playing, and his eyes became threatening.

"What do you want?"

The man took off his cap.

"Zio Efix!" the boy shouted, and began playing again, talking and laughing at the same time. "You aren't dead? Some said you were in America and had got sick, and that you sent a lot of money to your women. Now I'm the guardian here. If I wanted to chase you off like a thief I could do. But I won't. Want a grape? Take one. My *padrone,* Don Predu, doesn't care about this piece of land. He's got so many other farms. The big one, Badde Saliche – that one's productive. Don Predu gives the fruit from here to his cousins, the Pintor women. But they stay shut up in their house like a hedgehog in its hole. Oh, Zio Efix, I've got to tell you something. The other night – I stay in the hut at night, because I'm afraid of spirits, and always hear grandmother scratching at the door – the other night a scary thing happened! I felt a soft thing running over my feet. I yelled, I broke out in a sweat. But then at dawn I saw it was a wounded rabbit. Yes, it had managed to get away from a trap and it was here with its broken paw and looked at me with its two eyes like a human. I bandaged its paw, but then it got a fever. It burned in my hands like fire. Then it turned black and died."

Efix was sitting in front of the hut looking off into the distance.

"What do you think," he asked seriously. "Will Don Predu take me back?"

The boy became threatening again.

"And then he'd have to kick me out? What would I do? Grixenda will get married and move away. What can I do? Go begging? No, you go away, you're old."

"You're right," Efix said, and bowed his head. But his submissiveness made the little servant more benevolent.

"Don Predu is so rich that he can take you on, too. He can send you to other farms, because I like staying here. This is a pretty place. Grixenda says so, too."

"What's Grixenda doing?"

"She's making her wedding dress."

"Tell me, Zuannantoni. Has Don Giacinto come to town?"

"My future brother-in-law," the boy said with pride, "came this July. Grixenda was always sick. A little more and she would have died. Yes, he came...."

He was silent, with his face bent over his accordion, his eyes grave with memories.

"Tell me everything. You can tell me, Zuannantò. I'm like family."

"Yes, I'll tell you. Well, then, Grixenda was sick. She was wasting away like a wick. At night she had fever and would get up like a crazy woman and say: I want to go to Nuoro. But when she tried to open the door she couldn't. You understand: it was grandmother outside who pushed against the door and kept her from going. Then, once, I went to Nuoro. I found my brother-in-law in a place that seemed like hell: in the Mill. I told him everything. Then he asked for three days leave and came back with me. He rented a horse, because it cost less than a carriage, and took me on the back. It was so nice to go like that; it seemed like we were giants. He asked Grixenda to be his wife, and so by the Saints they are getting married."

"Who was the go-between?"

"I don't know. He asked Grixenda himself."

"Tell me, Zuannantoni, did Don Giacinto go see his aunts, my *padrone*?"

The boy hesitated again. "Yes," he then said. "He went there. I think they quarreled because he came out with red eyes like he had been crying. Grixenda looked at him and laughed, but through her teeth. He said: this is the last time they'll see me."

Efix asked no more questions. He spent the night in the hut and, because a big wind came up and the reeds on the ridge moaned like wounded animals, frightening the little guardian, Efix began to tell Bible stories, imitating the blind man's tone.

"Yes, there was a king who told his people that trees are spirits, and had his people adore them – and animals and fire, too. Then the true God was offended and made the king's servants so wicked they conspired to kill their master. Yes, he had made them worship a god of gold. That's why love for money is in the world, and relatives even kill relatives for money. Even innocent souls adore money."

Then he began to describe King Solomon's temple and his palaces. Zuannantoni fell asleep and Efix kept talking. Outside, the reeds on the ridge rustled so violently that it sounded like a battle.

In fact, when Efix left the hut at dawn, he saw hundreds of them hanging broken, their long leaves scattered on the ground like broken swords. And it seemed like the survivors, themselves stripped a little bare, bent over to look at their dead companions, caressing their wounded leaves.

"Take some grapes, Zio Efix," the boy told him, saying good-by thoughtfully. "If Don Predu sends you back here I'll be glad, because we can pass the time telling stories. Go over to Grixenda's."

And so Efix went back up the road toward town. The dawn was almost cold and the white hills looked snow covered. The little hills behind the villages scattered over the plain beyond the Castle smoked like smothered coals. Everything was silent and dead in the rosy morning. But Efix's spirits rose, and he felt like he was the prodigal son returning after all hope was gone.

He went straight to the usurer and laughed when he realized that even though she didn't recognize him immediately she welcomed him warmly, believing him to be a stranger, a servant sent by some property owner to ask for money.

"Kallina, darn it all, don't you recognize me? You're not the same either, you know."

She was holding her shoes, and let them fall one after the other. Then she bent over to pick them up.

"Efix, you see? You've turned out just like I swore you would! Even your clothes are different. Remember you wanted to kill me once."

"There's still time, if you don't stop! Tell me, how are you?"

"Not very well. For a long time I've had a headache. And pains and sleepless nights have worn me down like this – small, stooped, as though a vampire had sucked my blood."

"That's only just," thought Efix, but he didn't say so.

"The headaches are something awful, Efix. I've even made a vow to go on a pilgrimage to the church of San Francesco in October...."

"Listen," Efix said, who had sat down next to the *focolare* and was making no move to leave. It's no good going on a pilgrimage. If you have to do penance, do it in your own home."

"I don't have to do penance! If I go, I'll go out of devotion. My soul is before God and not before a sinner like you."

He hung his head.

"Listen," he began again, "I need clothes and money. You've got to help me, Kallina. You can if you want to. I'm like a soldier who's been to war. I'm back, but I can't keep these clothes."

"Tell me at least, where have you been?"

"I wanted to see a little bit of the world. I went as far as the Orient to see King Solomon's temple and house...that house is all gold...and the plates and vases are gold, even the keys and door frames are gold...."

The woman looked up at him through half-closed eyes while she put new laces in her shoes. She'd save the old ones because they'd be good to tie something. Why did he talk like that, like a beggar would? Was he making fun of her or did he have a fever?

"Efix, dear, going around the world has worn out your shoes and your brain!"

Nevertheless she loaned him the money, but he didn't leave.

"I can't leave and let Don Predu's sneering servants see me like this. You've got to get me some clothes. Come on, what do you think about when you're not sleeping? Come on, even you are human."

"Really, me too? More human than you, my dear. I never left my house to run around the world in my old age...."

"If you don't stop I'll take the club to you, Kallì, watch out!"

For the rest of the day they continued to insult each other, half jokingly, half seriously. But in the afternoon she went out to buy a nearly new costume from a woman whose husband had gone to America.

Toward evening Efix went to his *padrone*. Yes, toward evening, just like after a day off spent wandering around lazy and bored. Everything was quiet and sad up there. Monte loomed above the dark house in the greenish twilight sky, the new moon fell on it, the evening star trembled above the moon.

The front door was closed. Grass grew along the wall and on the steps like in front of an abandoned house. Efix was afraid to knock.

He saw Grixenda in her little doorway that shone like a golden rectangle against the black wall, and he remembered what Zuannantoni had said.

Grixenda stood in front of a fire drying her wet skirts. She was barefoot and her straight legs shone like bronze. When she saw the man she dropped her skirts and laughed, shouting in joyful recognition.

"What, Grixenda! You still go to the river? Don Giacinto allows it?"

"Doesn't *he* work? Or is he a *signore*? If he were a *signore* I would be underground.... Oh, well, aren't you coming in? Sit down. Is that *bisaccia* heavy? Is it full of gold? You've made your fortune on the sly, wicked as you are!"

He sat down and put his *bisaccia* on the ground. He looked at Grixenda and Grixenda looked at him mischievously, letting him understand that she knew the truth.

"But even we, Zio Efix, even we – Giacinto and I – will do something. We can become rich, too, Zio Efix. Who knows? Everything is possible in this world. I believe anything is possible."

"Aren't you already rich? Who's richer than you are?"

She bent over him, graceful and childlike, as she had once.

"That's what I've always said! When your *padrone* didn't want Giacinto and me to marry because I was poor, I said: aren't I young? Don't I love him? Are Noemi and Don Predu, with all they have, richer than we are? In years, yes, if nothing else!"

Efix started. "Are they getting married?"

"Yes, they're getting married! He was wasting away, like I was last spring. They said he was under a spell. Yes, he was under a spell! A spell of love. He even went to Oliena to visit a sorcerer. Finally, last week he went to the Madonna of Gonare on a pilgrimage, and made an offer of three scudi for a miracle. At least so the gossips say!"

Efix looked thoughtfully at the ground between his knees.

"Must I go back?" he asked himself. "Will they think the wind of good fortune brought me back?"

And suddenly, for a moment, he was sorry Noemi had accepted before he came back. But he immediately got up, humbly repentant. Ah, how he still sinned!

"Do you think Don Predu is there?" he asked, turning before leaving.

"I'm here, not there, Zio Efix!" Grixenda said, going up to him smiling. "And I can't say, because your *padrone* double lock the door when they see me!"

He went away, his heart beating wildly again. And it felt like his knocks on the door reverberated through his very being.

XVI

It was Noemi who opened the door. Efix saw her appear before him against the grayish background of the courtyard, very tall, thin, white faced: Lia as a girl, Lia resurrected.

She looked him over before letting him come in, like one looks at a stranger, then she only said: "Oh, it's you?" But this expression of suspicious and ironic surprise was enough to increase his humiliation and distress.

"Ah, well, I've come back, Donna Noemi," he said entering and following her across the courtyard. "The vagabond has returned. How is Donna Ester? May I see her?"

In the grayish dusk he saw everything in its place. The balcony above, black against the gray background of the wall, the well with red flowers, the rope railing on the stairway.

There was light in the kitchen, but not the blazing light there was in Grixenda's house. A gloomy light above the ancient bench in the middle of a large shadow.

No, nothing had changed. Everything was still dead. And Efix thought sorrowfully: "It must not be true that Donna Noemi gave her consent."

Instinctively he tried to hang his *bisaccia* on the peg, but the peg wasn't there. No one had replaced it and he held on to his *bisaccia* like a guest who must soon leave.

Donna Ester was quietly reading as she sat on a stool in front of the ancient bench, but suddenly the cat resting in its own shadow next to the lamp, following the movement of her hands with his eyes, jumped on her lap as though wanting to hide, and from there leaped under the bench. Ester looked up, saw the stranger, and began to stare at him with shining eyes, and the book shook in her hands.

"Well, then, yes, it's me, *padrona mia*! I've come back. The vagabond has returned. What do you say about that, Donna Ester? How have you been?"

"Efix! Efix! Efix!" she babbled.

"Efix himself! Are your eyes so bad that you need spectacles, Donna Ester?"

"You, Efix! Sit down. Yes, my eyes are bad after so much crying."

Noemi looked at them both with her wicked eyes and seemed to be enjoying the scene. "Yes, Ester! You have spectacles because you are old now. Sit down," she also invited Efix, patting her hand on the bench, and Efix sat next to his old mistress who was trembling with surprise. At first they didn't know what to say. He hugged his *bisaccia* to him and bent his head in shame. She took off her spectacles, closed them within the pages of her book, and seemed to want to lean against the servant.

Finally they both turned and looked at each other, and she shook her head reproachfully.

"Fine thing! You travel all around and have come back! But why not a line, a greeting? People come here even from America!"

Efix opened his mouth to answer, but he looked at Noemi who was laughing as if she knew the truth, and he remained silent, more humiliated than ever.

"And the way you went away, Efix! As if we had offended you, without saying a word. Efix! Just think about it. I kept saying to myself, Why did Efix do that? Will you finally tell us why?"

"Things of the world! You get old and feeble minded," he answered with a vague gesture. "Now I'm here.... Let's don't talk about it any more."

"Now, what do you expect to do? Will you return to Predu? Or, like people say, is it true you've become rich? But why don't you put that *bisaccia* down? At least have a bite to eat here."

"I have to go, Donna Ester.... I just came to say hello."

"You'll stay here until tomorrow," Noemi said, and with an almost feline gesture she took his *bisaccia* and put it down on the bench.

They looked at each other, and he understood the two of them had to talk, to resume an interrupted discussion.

"Efix, listen, at least tell us what you've been doing since you never wrote. How many things you'll have to tell us now. Oh, Efix, Efix, who would have believed you'd go on a trip around the world at your age!"

"Better late than never, Donna Ester! But there's not much to tell."

"Tell us that much...."

"All right, yes, I'll tell you...."

Noemi set the table silently. There was the same basket blackened by time, polished by use, the same kind of bread and food to go with it. Efix ate and talked, with stumbling words veiled with timid lies; but when he had thrown his crumbs and the last dregs of his glass on the floor – since the ground always wants its little part of man's nourishment – he straightened his back a little and his eyes were encircled with beaming wrinkles.

"Well, then all of us travelers were poor devils. We kept on going without knowing where we would end up, but always hoping to earn a little money. We went in a file, like prisoners...."

"But didn't you go by sea?"

"By sea, yes, what am I saying? And on stormy seas, too. I got soaked many times. We didn't go hungry, no. Who was hungry? Not me. Sometimes I felt like a hand had grabbed my stomach and wanted to tear it out. Then I would eat and feel better. Once we got there we started working.

"What work?"

"Oh, easy work; we took dirt from one place and put it in another...."

"Is it true they're making a canal to pass to the sea? But doesn't water come inside the canal?"

"Yes, it comes inside the canal; but there are machines to keep it back. They're like pumps.... I don't know how to describe them to you, though!"

Noemi was listening quietly, stroking the cat that purred with pleasure in her lap. She listened, but her thoughts were far away.

"Were you right in the country? They say everything is very expensive there. Remember what the emigrants said at the Church of the Rimedio? And then, they say it's a town where you can't have a good time."

"Oh, you can have a good time! Whoever wants to enjoy himself, understand! Some play music, some dance, some pray, some get drunk. And then everyone goes away...."

"They go away? Where?"

"I mean...to their barracks, to rest."

"What language do they speak?"

"Language? Every language. I spoke Sardinian with my companions...."

"Oh, you had Sardinian companions?"

"Yes, some Sardinian companions. An old man and a young one. I seem to still have them by my side – except for the respect due you ladies."

Noemi eyes shone wickedly. "I hope we're cleaner!" she said, squeezing his arm.

"Yes, an old man and a young man. They were always fighting. They were mean, envious, jealous, but basically good. Man is made like that: good and bad. And yet always unlucky. Even rich men are often unlucky. Oh, yes!"

The squeeze from Noemi reminded him of the squeeze from Giacinto there in the courtyard at Nuoro, and the secret that kept the woman from accepting Don Predu's request.

"Don Predu, for example," he said almost involuntarily. Then he added, looking at his young mistress, "isn't he rich and unlucky?"

But his mistress laughed again, and he was irritated in spite of himself.

"What's there to laugh about? Oh, so Don Predu isn't unlucky? Until you take pity on him, Donna Noemi.... And yet he's a good man."

Then Donna Ester got up, leaned her hand on the back of the bench and stood looking at them severely.

"What do you mean, good," Noemi said, but she wasn't laughing. "He's old, now, and can't make fun of his neighbors anymore: that's all there is to it! Let's not talk about him."

"No, let's talk about him," Ester said heatedly. "Efix, explain what you mean."

"What must I explain, Donna Ester? That Don Predu wants to marry Donna Noemi?"

"Oh, you know about that? How did you know?"

"I was the first go-between."

"The first and the last," Noemi shouted throwing the cat down like a ball of yarn. "That's enough. I don't want to talk about it any more."

However, Efix was obstinate.

"That's because I never gave him your answer, Donna Noemi! How could I go tell him? I didn't dare, and that's why I ran away."

Donna Ester sat down beside him again, and he felt her trembling.

"Oh, Efix," she murmured. "He had the idea back then and you didn't say anything? And you ran away? But why? As I live and breathe, it all seems like a dream. I never knew anything: only what people came to tell me, outsiders. And you, my sister, and you...and you...."

"What should I have told you, Ester? Did he ever ask me? When did he ever explain himself? He sends presents, he comes sometimes, he sits down and talks with you and hardly says a word to me. Have I ever sent him away?"

"You don't send him away, but you do something even worse. You laugh when he comes. You make fun of him."

"It's only right! You harvest what you sow."

"Noemi, why do you say things like that? You've seemed strange for some time! You're not reasonable any more. Why do you say he makes fun of you if he sent someone to tell you he loves you?"

"He sent a servant to tell me!"

Ester looked at Efix, but Efix was silent, head down, as in the past when his mistresses argued. He was waiting, on the other hand, certain that Noemi, in spite of her contempt, had to take up the subject again between the two of them alone.

"Efix, hear how she talks? I'll tell you that you haven't been the only one to tell her. Even Giacinto...."

But this name released a frightening void between them, and Efix saw Noemi shudder, livid with anger and hate.

"Ester!" she said harshly. "You swore not to speak his name again."

And she went out as though suffocating with rage.

"Yes," murmured Ester, bending toward Efix. "She hates him to the point that she made me swear never to mention his name again. When he came the last time to tell us that he was marrying Grixenda and to advise Noemi to accept Predu, she sent him away as terrible as you just saw her. And he went away crying. But tell me, tell me, Efix," she went on sadly, "haven't we had bad luck? Giacinto ruins us and marries that beggar and, on the other hand, Noemi refuses a good opportunity. But why, Efix, tell me, you've been around the world. Is it like this everywhere? Why does fate break us like this, like reeds?"

"Yes," he then said, "we're just like reeds in the wind, Donna Ester. That's why! We are reeds, and fate is the wind."

"Yes, all right. But why this fate?"

"Why the wind? Only God knows why."

"Then may His will be done," she said, resting her head on her chest. Seeing her so bent, so old and sad, Efix felt almost strong. To comfort her he thought of telling her one of the blind man's many stories.

"Besides, no one's ever satisfied. Do you know the story of the Queen of Sheba? She was beautiful and had a kingdom far away, with many gardens of figs and pomegranates and a palace all of gold. Well, then, she heard that King Solomon was richer than she was and she couldn't sleep. Envy was eating her so bad she wanted to go there to see it even if she had to go 'cross half the world...."

Ester bent a little in the other direction and took the book containing her glasses.

"Those stories are in here. It's the Holy Bible."

Efix looked humbly at the book and didn't continue.

Once left alone, he stretched out on the mat, but in spite of his deep weariness he couldn't sleep. He had the impression that the blind men were lying there next to him, and that outside in the shadows stretched an unknown country. His *padrone,* however, were there on the bench looking at him: Donna Ester, old and almost pleading; Donna Noemi, smiling, but more terrible than when she was stern.

And, strangely enough, he no longer felt uneasy with Donna Ester or afraid of Donna Noemi. He was truly like the freed slave become rich, visiting his former owners.

"I can help them, I can still help them, even if they don't want me to.... Tomorrow...."

He was waiting anxiously for tomorrow. That was why he couldn't sleep. Tomorrow he would talk with Noemi. They would continue the conversation interrupted so many months before, and perhaps he'd be able to take good news to Don Predu.

He began to pray softly, then louder until he seemed to be singing like the pilgrims up at the Madonna del Miracolo.

Tomorrow.... Everything will be all right tomorrow. Everything will be settled, everything cleared up. He believed he finally understood why God had urged him to leave his *padrone*'s house and to go around like a vagabond. It was to give Giacinto time to find his conscience, and Noemi time to heal her torment.

"If I had given Don Predu her answer right away everything would have been over," he thought with a sense of relief, and as soon as he went to sleep he began to dream. A faint light illuminates the surrounding plain, a white ring above a large black circle. Sunrise. The blind men get up, entwine their fingers, bend over in front of him and have him sit on their hands and put his arms around their neck. They lift him up, carry him away, far away, singing like children do in their games.

He laughed. He had never been so happy. But in the background, in the dark kitchen, Donna Ester and Donna Noemi didn't move from the bench, and he felt embarrassment for one and fear for the other. Then he closed his eyes and pretended to be blind himself. And so all three went here and there over soft ground, singing sacred hymns of the Holy Spirit. But a hand grasped his coat from behind and stopped them. Startled, he threw himself down. Opening his eyes and saw Donna Noemi with a lantern in her hand.

"Were you already asleep, Efix? I'm sorry, but Ester told me that you'd be leaving early in the morning and I came back down."

He sat upright quickly on the mat. Next to his feet she stood straight, still, tall with the lantern in hand. They were surrounded by a circle of shadow outside a ring of light, like in his dream.

"I wanted to talk to you alone, Efix. Ester doesn't understand certain things. You were wrong to talk with her. You don't understand either."

He was silent. He understood, yes, but he had to be quiet and pretend, like a slave.

"You don't understand and so you talk too much, Efix! If you had just brought me the message that day without giving me advice, it would have been better. Instead we said many pointless things. Now I want to know if it's true that you didn't say anything to Predu about our discussion."

"Nothing, Donna Noemi, never!"

"Another thing I want to ask, Efix; but you must tell me the truth. Have you...." She hesitated a moment, then raised her voice, "have you told Giacinto anything about this? Tell me the truth."

"No," he lied in a firm voice. "I swear to you, I didn't talk to him about it."

"Then you think it was Predu who told him?"

"I believe so, Donna Noemi."

"Another thing. Tell me, why did you go away?"

"I don't know. I was just wondering about that before I went to sleep. I think it was the Lord who made me leave. I was afraid and ashamed to go to Don Predu with that answer. Yes, Donna Noemi, because I know Don Predu had taken me into his service just for that. He loved you and wanted me to be the intermediary. Then, when you said no, I ran away...."

Noemi began to laugh. But an easy laugh, not like the mean laugh earlier. It was compassion for Efix, compassion for Don Predu, but also satisfaction and sweetness. Never, never had Efix heard her laugh like that. He would remember that laugh, that face bent over him, that shadow and that tremulous light around them. And his heart would pound as though it would break.

Lia as she was the night of her escape was standing before him.

"Another thing and then enough. Listen, do you think Giacinto will really marry Grixenda?"

"Yes, it's a sure fact."

"When will they get married?"

"Before Christmas."

She lowered the lantern, as though to see his face better, and so illuminated hers as well. How pale she was, and how old and young her face was at the same time!

Pride, passion, longing – to destroy her miserable old life and build another newer and stronger one with the pieces – burned in her eyes.

"Listen to me, Efix," she said raising the lantern. "So now you can tell Predu that I accept him. But we must marry immediately – before those two."

XVII

Once more Efix was down there on the farm. Summer had ended, the fruit was harvested, and Zuannantoni, given the chore of pasturing a flock of sheep near the village, went willingly.

And now Efix is again sitting in his usual place in front of the hut below the blue-gray stand of reeds. The sky is red over the white hill; the wind is blowing and the reeds tremble and whisper: "Efix, remember? Remember? You went away, you came back, you're with us again, like one of us. Some bend, some break, some hold out today, but will bend tomorrow and break the day after tomorrow. Efix, remember? Remember?"

He was weaving a mat and praying. From time to time a sharp pain in his side made him straighten up, as rigid as if someone had stuck his kidneys with an iron pole. He would then bend over, livid and trembling, like a reed in the wind. But after the spasm he would feel a great weakness, a deep sweetness, because he hoped to die soon. His time was over.

As long as he could, he would stay there on the land that had drained off all his strength and all his tears.

Autumn came with October's sweet days, then the first cold of November. The mountains facing him and those beyond the valley seemed volcanos: clouds of smoke plowed by pale flames.

Toward evening the sky cleared. All the silver from all the mines in the world was piled in blocks heaped on the horizon. Invisible workers constructed houses, buildings, entire cities, and then destroyed them immediately. The ruins grew white in the twilight, covered with golden grass and pink shrubs. Herds of gray and black horses went by, and a yellow point shone behind a dismantled castle that looked like a fire from a hermit's or bandit's hideout up there. The moon was breaking through.

Slowly it illuminated the whole mysterious landscape, and as though touched by a magical finger, everything disappeared. A blue lake flooded the horizon. The clear cold autumn night, with great stars in the sky and distant fires on the earth, extended from the mountains to the sea. In the silence the river roared like the blood of the sleepy valley. Efix felt death approaching little by little, as though rising silently up the path accompanied by a procession of wandering spirits, by the *panas* beating clothes down at the river, by the light flutter of innocent souls transformed into leaves, into flowers....

One night he was dozing in his hut when he woke up suddenly, as if someone had shaken him.

It seemed like a mysterious being fell on him, stabbing his guts with a knife, and that all his blood spurted from his lacerated body, flooding his mat, bathing his hair, face, hands.

Efix began to shout as if he were really being murdered, but only the murmur of water answered him in the night.

He was afraid and thought of going back to town, but for long hours in the night he was too weak to move, as though bloodless. A deathly sweat soaked his body.

At dawn he moved. This time he really would go and he put everything in order: the farm tools at the back, the mat rolled up beside them, the pan upside down on the board, the bundle of rushes in the corner, the *focolare* swept. Everything in order, like a good servant who goes away and wants to make a favorable impression on the one taking his place.

He took up his *bisaccia*, picked a jasmine from the bush and looked around. The whole valley looked white and sweet as the jasmine.

All was silence. The phantoms had retreated behind the veil of dawn and even the water murmured more softly as if to let Efix' footsteps sound louder on the path. Only the reeds stirred above on the ridge, straight and rigid as swords sharpening themselves on the metal of the sky.

"Good-by, Efix, good-by."

He returned to his *padrone* and lay down on a mat.

"It's a good thing you came here," said Ester, covering him with a blanket; and Noemi also bent over him, feeling his pulse, pulling on his arm in an attempt to get him in a bed.

"Leave me here, Donna Noemi," he groaned with a smile, but with eyes vague like a blind man's already covered with the veil of death. "My place is here."

Later a new attack made him writhe and grow dark in the face; while the women sent for the doctor he began to rave.

The kitchen filled with phantoms and the terrible being that wouldn't stop hitting him shouted in his ear: "Confess! Confess!"

Ester also kneeled beside the mat murmuring: "Efix, my dear, do you want me to call Father Paskale? He'll read you the Gospel and that will raise your spirits...."

But Efix looked fixedly at her, with glassy eyes in his blackened face shining with drops of sweat; terror of the end was suffocating him. He was afraid his soul would suddenly flee from his body, just as he had fled from his mistresses' house, and banished from the world of the just, he would wander about restless and damned with the phantoms of the valley; and he answered definitely not. He didn't want the priest. More than fear of death and damnation was his fear of revealing his secret.

And here was Don Predu, sitting next to the mat and beginning to make jokes. Don Predu was happy. He was fat again and the gold chain didn't hang so far down his black waistcoat.

"Why did you come back here, you old fool? Would you be so bad off at my house? You're like the cat that comes back even after it's carried off in a sack. Come on, let's go. I'll put you in Stefana's bed."

Noemi, bent over with a smoking dish in her hand while she dried the sweat on his face, attempted the same tone as her big fiancé, "Come on, drink. Do you want to die a bachelor?"

"Well, then," Efix said raising his head but refusing the broth, "let's go...."

"What are you saying? You want to go on the road again? What a gadabout...."

"Oh, what are you doing? Let's go to Stefana who's saved a pomegranate for you.... Get up, boy!"

But Efix lay back down and closed his eyes – not because he was offended by their teasing, but because he felt so far from them, from everyone. Far away, ever further, but weighed down, with a load that wouldn't let him to go on or turn back. It was worse than when he had to lead the blind men.

Finally the doctor arrived. He touched him everywhere, beat the knuckles of his fingers on his belly as hard as a drum, turned him, turned him again, tossed the blanket over him like fermenting bread.

"It's your liver playing a bad joke. You have to go to bed, Efix."

The sick man raised a finger to gesture no.

"As long as I have to die, let me die a servant."

"Before God we're neither servants nor *padroni*," Ester said; and Don Predu tried to lift him in his arms.

"Be quiet, fool. Quiet!"

Efix began moaning, shaking weakly like a wounded bird still trying to fly. "You want to kill me before my time...."

Then the doctor made a gesture with his hand and raised his eyes skyward, and Don Predu lay the sick man back down and didn't joke anymore.

They left him there. Hours and days went by, and in his delirium Efix dreamed he was walking with the blind men toward valleys and the *tancas* of high plains, and he dreamed about the festivals, coins falling down on him, and pious women, handsome men on white-footed horses running along the side of Monte who pelted coins and biting words at him from a distance.

But the high smoky walls with red spots of copper and the bench in the background cut off the horizon. Beyond that he didn't go, but he needed to – to get free of his burden, to heal his pain.

Twice Noemi found him up trying to go out into the courtyard. They removed the key from the door.

Ester bent over him, straightened his pillow and the blanket covering him, and felt his pulse.

"Efix, the Rector could come visit you."

Eyes closed, he lifted a finger to indicate no.

The first days some asked to see him, but Noemi barely opened the door and sent everyone away. From inside he heard. That people would remember him, so far away and at the edge of the world, surprised and moved him.

One morning he asked Ester, "Who came to see me a bit ago?"

"That was Zuannantoni."

"If he comes back, Donna Ester, please let him come in.... It's time to start saying good-bye...."

"What are you saying, Efix! Why this fixation? Let the Rector come. He would read the Gospel and you wouldn't be afraid of dying anymore...."

He didn't answer. No, they weren't trying to fool him, but his hour hadn't come yet, and he held on to life only because he was afraid of laying down his burden in his mistresses' house.

Life around him took on a new aspect. A wave of joy seemed to invade the house when Don Predu arrived, and there were Donna Ester's timid laughs, the couple's discussions, plans, gossip, sudden silences out of respect for the sick man.

Then he felt he was an obstacle and wanted to leave.

One morning Ester, who slept on the ground floor to watch over him, got up early and put everything in order while she talked to herself under her breath. Bending over him with a cup of milk, she said: "Come on, Efix, cheer up! Today Predu will decide the wedding day. Are you happy?"

He nodded yes. Then he covered his head with the blanket and under it he felt like he was already dead, but just the same rejoicing for the good fortune of his *padrone*.

Noemi got up early also. She talked with her sister, saying with fierce pride: "Why must he set the date and not me? I'm no little town girl to follow common custom."

"Why are you so impatient? The bans have been published. Today he'll talk about the rest."

Noemi was agitated and Efix heard her coming and going through the house with a light but restless step. Finally she sat by the door and sewed silently. When Don Predu arrived she moved the chair, making way for him, but barely looked at him and answered his greeting with a slight nod. Ester came down the stairs at once to act as an interpreter for the couple for whom misunderstandings often arose because everything offended Noemi who took everything wrong in spite of Don Predu's good will.

As soon as he came in he went to Efix and stood looking down on him. "How's it going? All right, it seems to me. Let's get up!"

Efix raised indifferent, sunken eyes, and as Don Predu bent over to touch him, he put out his hand as though to fend off the powerful body that brushed his disintegrating one. "Go away...."

And Don Predu went to sit next to his fiancée. "What kind of mood are we in today?"

"Watch out, Predu, don't pull my embroidery, you'll make me stick myself...."

"That's what I want to do!"

"Predu, leave me alone. You're behaving like a child!"

"It's your fault because you've cast a spell over me...."

"Predu, stop it!"

"Do you know what that philosopher Stefana says? She says you've now reversed the charm: first to make me lose weight, now to make me fat."

"You're joking, Predu, but your servant is a backbiter."

"But it's obvious that I'm gaining weight. There's no way to break the spell.... "

Ester leaned on Noemi's chair and looked at her cousin without a word, waiting. Then he looked up at her, slapped his knees and said: "Well, when do we want to break this chain?"

"That's for you to decide, Predu."

Noemi continued sewing. She looked up with shining eyes, but soon lowered them without a word.

"Ester, I would say before Advent."

"Good. Before Advent."

"Do you think everything can be ready toward the middle of the month?"

"Everything will be ready, Predu."

"Fine, fine."

Silence. Noemi sewed, Donna Ester looked at her over her shoulder. Finally, Don Predu asked almost timidly: "And you, what do you say?"

"Who are you talking to?"

"Noemi!" protested Ester; however, the man motioned to her to be quiet, and he began to pull the sewing from his fiancée's knee.

"Let's talk about the spell! How to undo it before I get too fat. How do you think it can be undone? Like this, like this! To your health whoever sees us."

And between Ester's forced laughter and Noemi's protests, he held her by the shoulders and gave her a loud kiss.

Under his blanket Efix was thinking, "How happy I am! Now I can die." But he felt unable to go, unable to leave that circle of walls locking him in.

Don Predu stayed there all day, invited to dinner by his cousins. He talked, laughed, joked; however, every once in a while he was silent, because Noemi seemed to take little notice of him. A grave silence then surrounded Efix, and he understood he was an obstacle, a burden and worry to the women and to Don Predu himself.

He had to *go away*, leave the couple free to love each other and joke without that image of death before them.

And suddenly, there in the dark, under the cover, he thought he understood why he was unable to leave. Something was still keeping him there in his *padrone*'s house, like an account yet unsettled, that needed to be settled.

And when Ester, thinking he was asleep, bent over him and lightly raised the edge of the blanket, she saw him with his eyes wide open, his face red, his lips trembling.

"Efix, Efix, what's wrong?"

He motioned with his eyes to come nearer and murmured in a weak voice: "Donna Ester, please, if you will, call Father Paskale."

After his confession he spoke no more, he moaned no longer. He remained with his head covered, but each time Donna Ester raised the blanket she saw his poor face grown smaller, purplish, wrinkled like a dried prune. One evening he opened his eyes, looking at her with his frightened look that awoke such pity in her, and murmured in a voiceless way: "It's long, Donna Ester! I'm sorry."

"What's long, Efix?"

"The road.... You never get there!"

In fact, he always seemed to be walking. He went up a mountain, crossed a *tanca*; but after reaching its boundary there was another mountain, another plain, and behind it the sea.

However, now he was walking tranquilly, and was only sorry he wasn't getting there in order to remove his body from the women's house. But one day, or night – he didn't know what time it was any more – he seemed to have gone as far as the low wall of the little farm, up high on the embankment of reeds, and he stretched out heavily on the rocks. The reeds rustled, bending to touch him, lapping at him with leaves that were like live things with fingers, tongues. They spoke to him, and one stuck in his ear so he could hear better. It was a mysterious murmur that repeated the whispering of the phantasms in the valley, the voice of the river, the psalms of the pilgrims, the palpitation of the Mill, the moan of Zuannantoni's accordion. He listened, gripping the wall face down, and on one side he saw the women's kitchen and on the other a foggy expanse like up there from Monte Gonare.

Donna Ester climbed up from the valley with her face covered by a black wing; she waved the wing, showing her dark, sorrowful face, her eyes veiled with pity, but she drew back behind the wall as though afraid of falling. And other figures came up there, all with their faces hidden behind a black wing, and all came close, but drew back immediately, frightened by the danger of falling into the beyond.

Efix knew all these people, heard them speak, knew they were alive and real. And yet he had the impression of dreaming. They were figures of his life's dream.

It was the priest, it was Milese, it was Zuannantoni, they were Don Predu's servants, Don Predu himself and Noemi. At times one of them got the courage to try to help him, to drag him down from the wall, without success.

He began to get annoyed with them and turned away to look at the foggy valley. And then the fog began to clear. Spots of golden woods appeared between rents in the blue, and on the ridge above him a pomegranate tree like the one the blind man talked about bent its heavy limbs of split red fruit letting the pearl globes fall.

But the people beyond the wall didn't leave him in peace to contemplate such good. He didn't look around any longer, except one day when a hand rested on his shoulder and a voice calling softly in his ear startled him. "Efix! Efix!"

Giacinto's face, his sweet eyes damp with pity, stood over him. Among so many dead figures that one seemed the only one still alive, so alive that his hot hands almost had the power to pull him up, to put him back into this world.

But only for a moment. Then even this figure was veiled, lost power, turned back into a phantom; and Efix felt sad, as if Giacinto were dying and not he.

"Efix, come on! What are you doing? Won't you talk to me? I came for you, you know. I'm here. They didn't want to let me in, but I jumped over the wall. Come on, look at me!"

He looked at him with eyes that no longer saw.

"Aunt Noemi ran away when she saw me! She'll never forgive me! Tell me, what did she say? That she never wants to see me again? That she swore never to speak my name? I don't know. But that's not important. I'm happy they're getting married. Do you know what happened the last time I came? I said to her: 'Get married, Zia Noemi. Zio Pietro's rich, he loves you, he'll make you happy.' She looked at me with contempt, and I realized she would never agree to it. Then, Efix, listen – let's speak softly so they won't hear – well, then, I remembered your advice. I looked her in the eye and said: 'Zia Noemi, I'll marry Grixenda, because only Grixenda, poor like me, young and alone like me, can be my companion.' Then Noemi turned pale as death. She was afraid of me and I went away. I was crying. Did she tell you? Come on, Efix, you aren't listening. Come on! Here's Zia Ester. Isn't it true, Zia Ester, that Efix is pretending to be sick so he won't have to come to my wedding and Zia Noemi's and bring a present? And yet they say you brought back money from your journey...."

Efix heard the words and even understood them, but they were without sound, like written words.

"Come on, at least tell me what's wrong. You haven't even told me where you've been. Do you remember when you came to the Mill and I asked you where you were going? You said you were going to a good job. Don't you remember? Open your eyes, look at me. Where did you go?..."

Efix began to feel annoyed again. He opened his eyes for a moment and then closed them, already heavy with the sleep of death. Giacinto's words beyond the wall mixed with the rustling reeds, with the drone of the passing wind.

Then suddenly he seemed to revive. During the evening a violent attack had ground him like salt in a mortar. He had become deaf and mute with pain, but he had seen Don Predu look at Noemi with a gesture of discouragement. Because the wedding was set for the day after tomorrow, and if he died he would bring bad luck to them or cause them to postpone the wedding ceremony to another day. Then, in the depths of the darkness already wrapped round him, the will to combat death shone like a distant lamp.

He uncovered his face and spoke: "Donna Ester, I'm feeling better. Give me something to drink."

Both of the women ran to him and Noemi herself raised his head to let him drink. "Good, Efix! That's fine. Do you know what happens today?"

He motioned yes while drinking.

"You are happy, aren't you, Efix? How long have you thought about this day? It will seem like a dream."

He motioned yes, yes. Everything was a dream.

Then they left him alone because Noemi had to get dressed. He raised his head and looked around surreptitiously, continuing to make gestures of approval. Everything was fine. The wedding ceremony would take place in the bridegroom's house, and here nothing disturbed the ancient peace. Out of consideration for the sick man the kitchen had not been cleaned, as was customary for a wedding; the house and the courtyard were silent, the cat was motionless on the bench, black with green eyes like the idol of solitude. In the silence the screech of rotten wood on the balcony could be heard. Raising his head a little further Efix looked at the ruined wall and the grass and flowers of bones in the ancient cemetery for the last time.

But suddenly a figure appeared at the door: tall, slender, dressed in a fitted dress dotted with black flowers, a garland of roses on her head, and here and there on her face, body, feet something glittered: her eyes, jewels, shoes....

He opened his eyes wide and recognized Noemi. But behind her, straightening the roses on her hat and the folds of her dress, Donna Ester seemed like a shadow of the bride with the black wings of her shawl tossed back on her shoulders.

"I look all right, don't I?" asked Noemi standing before him, adjusting the sleeves. "Does this dress seemed too tight? It's the fashion. And look how pretty this is: it's a present from Predu."

In spite of her tight dress she bent over to show him the mother of pearl rosary with a large gold cross.

"See? It was an old bishop's cross. It belonged to Predu's grandmother, who was also ours. So it remains in the family. It's beautiful, isn't it? Look at the Christ, it seems like He's smiling while tears and blood flow down.... And in the back, look...."

Efix looked silently, motionless, with his dark dry hands grasping the hem of the blanket; and he seemed to be looking out from the other world to contemplate the happiness of his *padrone* one more time. But, bending even further, with bowed knees, so they were face to face, she said: "Look what a present, Efix!"

She was pale in her wine-red dress, her wicked eyes full of tears.

But they weren't a cause of pain for Efix. "We were born to suffer like Him. We must weep and be silent...." he said in a whisper. That was his wedding wish.

From that moment on he spoke not another word. He seemed to be hanging onto the hem of the blanket in order not to fall, and to be watching the world's spectacle from the height of the wall.

Then Don Predu and relatives came to take the bride away. They came in, ranged confusedly around the kitchen like figures in a dream, but with strange details in relief.

Don Predu was wearing a new black, close-fitting suit that forced him to breath hard, but Efix couldn't distinguish his face. He did see Milese's long, thin, sarcastic mouth, as though full of repressed laughter, and the swollen belly of one of the women's relatives who was to accompany the bride, and two candles with two pink ribbons held in two pale little hands.

Everyone was as serious as if they had come to take away his dead body and not the bride, and they walked around quietly so as not to bother him.

Ester, with her shawl loose and fluttering on her shoulders, lined up the procession: first the children with tall candles, then the bride with her relative, then the groom with his relatives, and finally the few invited guests. Milese seemed to be laughing at everyone silently in the rear.

"Now they'll leave me alone," Efix thought a little bitterly. "Alone. And it was me who did everything!"

At the door Noemi turned to wave good-bye with the gold cross. *Addio.* And, as had happened with Giacinto, he had the impression it was she who was dying.

They all went out. Donna Ester bent over him, seeming to cover him with her black wings.

"I'll come right back, as soon as I walk over with them. I have to go. Be quiet and lie still."

Yes, he lay still in his place. Still and alone. Zuannantoni's accordion could be heard playing in honor of the couple, and he began to remember so many things again: the noise of the Mill at Nuoro, the clouds over Monte Gonare, the reeds rustling on the ridge....

"Efix, remember? Efix, remember?"

How large the kitchen had become! Dark and warm, with the walls far away, with the mysterious background like a *tanca* at night. The nightingale sang, the blind man told a story about King Solomon's gold palace.

"...Everything was gold, like in the world of truth; everything was pure, shining. Gold pomegranates, gold vases, gold mats...."

And he saw Don Predu's house, with the pomegranates heavy with fruit, the palm trees, the mats covered with bunches of grapes and golden pumpkins.

"Noemi will be fine…there…she'll eat well, she'll get fat, she'll give money to Donna Ester to fix the balcony. She'll be fine.… She'll be like the Queen of Sheba. But not even the Queen of Sheba was happy.… Noemi will also get tired of her gold cross and will want to go far away, like Lia, like the Queen of Sheba, like everyone.…"

But this no longer amazed him; he needed to go far away, to other lands where things were greater than in ours.

And so he left. He closed his eyes and pulled the blanket over his head. And there he found himself once more on the wall of the little farm. The reeds were murmuring, Lia and Giacinto were sitting silently in front of the hut looking toward the sea.

He seemed to go to sleep. But suddenly he gave a start. He had the impression he had fallen off the low wall.

He had fallen off, into the valley of death.

Ester found him like that, quiet, under the blanket: very still.

She shook him, called him, and realizing he was dead and that they had let him die alone, she began to weep loudly, with a harsh moan that frightened her. She tried unsuccessfully to calm herself. Then she went to close the door so no one would surprise her mourning over a dead servant, and so people wouldn't know that the family had left him to die alone while they enjoyed an important celebration.

While waiting for the hours to go by, she moved the body, dry and light as a baby's, washed it, dressed it, speaking to him under her breath, between one prayer and another, telling him about the wedding, how Noemi was crying as she entered her rich new lodging – crying because she was so happy, you understand – how the house was full of presents, how people threw wheat and flowers as far as the courtyard to wish them good luck, how everyone was happy.

"And you did this…you went away like this, secretly…without saying anything…like the other time.… Oh, Efix, you shouldn't have done it…today, this very day!…"

He seemed to be listening with his glassy eyes half closed, calm but determined not to respond, like a good, respectful servant.

Remembering that he liked flowers, Ester plucked a geranium by the well and put it between his fingers on the crucifix. Finally she covered his body with a green silk rug they had brought out for the wedding. But the rug was small, and his feet remained uncovered, pointing toward the door, as was the custom. And it seemed that the servant was sleeping one last time in the noble house, resting before undertaking his journey toward eternity.

This Book Was Completed on October 15, 1998 at
Italica Press, New York, New York and
Was Set in Galliard. It Was Printed
On 60-lb Natural Paper by
Stanton Publication
Services, St. Paul,
Minnesota
U. S. A.
* *
*